DARK ANGEL

Part 1.

Sir Patrick Bijou

DARK ANGEL

I HAVE SOMETHING TO TELL

Sir Patrick Bijou is known for his role in the United Nations as a UN Ambassador for World Peace and a Senior Sovereign Redemption Judge for the International Court of Justice and International Criminal Courts. He is also a Fund Manager and dynamic Investment Banker.

Sir Patrick is an eclectic writer who lives in the United Kingdom and was born in Georgetown and raised in London, England.

His authorship has earned him fame because his publications are not limited to a genre or theme but from adventurous, thrilling, romantic, criminal, and dramatic theme fictional novels. However, his many experiences have influenced his diverse writing prowess.

In all his academic studies, though, the true treasures he took away are not the certificates (though those are very important), but instead, the experiences he had, the people he met, the foods he ate and even the places he stayed.

"In truth, I am a citizen of the world, and this greatly influences my writing., says Sir Patrick.

"So, if you are already a fan of mine, I appreciate you. If you are not yet one, then what are you waiting for? Read a book and then read some more. I create characters that resonate with you and infuse life into all he writes".

Finding his Books

Sir Patrick has written over 25 published fictional and non-fictional books across several genres and realises the need to make it easier for his readers to find his books.

www.sirpatrickbijou.com

Table of Contents

vii

CHAPTER 1

First let me say this Vampires and Druids exist, not only that they walk among you, living beneath the radar as it were, hidden from the humans that are scattered across the world, my kind is secretive, and only one rule exists that all must follow or else find ourselves on the end of a stake and that rule is to keep the secret.

My name is Dominic and I was turned in 1784 in Ireland by a vampire called Marcus, he found me dying in a gutter in Dublin with a knife wound to my chest, he drained the last dregs of my blood though I had already lost most of it through my chest and replaced it with his own, he was killed in 1946 in London, it left me alone in the world, I began to wander venturing around the world, I visited Europe and Asia on my search for companionship, I found myself in America finally, common myths about my kind state that we cannot walk in the sunlight this is a myth, all that sunlight does to us is weaken our abilities preventing us from using our full strength and speed and weakens our persuasive powers, in America I enrolled in high school, I was turned when I was 28 and have not aged since then, my physique is misleading I am Well-muscled, Dark Hair, Crystalline blue eyes but the blood that runs in my veins means that I could easily overpower almost anything or anyone, but I couldn't just go on a rampage in this internet world century.

Dominic's mate Abigayle died centuries ago. She was raped and murdered. They had stabbed me so many times, knowing what I was, that I could barely lift my head, let alone offer help. Even to my Abigayle. I laid face down on the floor, unable to lift my body as they raped her. The grief... no, the agony I felt at what they did to her, and anger at myself, because I could do nothing, has haunted me to this very day." He was quiet for a moment before continuing. "After they removed her head, they decided that I was too far gone to survive, so they left me to burn in the fire. Besides, it was daylight out, and they assumed there was no way for me to escape."

Although I own Club Viata, I had to stay hidden and always watch my identity to avoid being discovered, I decided to join a college with humans, The school at which I was enlisted was tedious but it is always interesting to see how humans react to stimuli specifically how the stupid females continually attempt to throw themselves at me, what all of them do not realize is that my tastes run on the more masculine side, some of my kind are like me and prefer the company of men to those of women, in my 228 years of life I took interest in few humans, and even then they did not hold my attention for long, at this school none of the humans here had taken my interest.

I walked to the school feeling the sun hit my flesh ignoring the slight irritation that the sunlight caused against my skin, the school was less than an hour away from my home, bought with the numerous amounts of money that I have accumulated for the 228 years that I have walked the earth, my skin was protected from burning so I have kept the pale complexion which I was born with, the humans that I noticed around the street paused to stare at me walk past, I saw one woman walking past and I flashed her a smile and chuckled as I heard her breathing stutter and listened as her heart sped up as she walked briskly away, I ran my fingers through my light brown hair and continued on my journey to the school.

I neared the school and sniffed breathing in the scents of the pupils feeling the slight ache in my throat as their scents mingled together culminating in a general aura of thirst, I overrode the urge using my 228 years of experience with the scent of human blood, one scent stood out from the others, I had memorized the various scents of the humans and I immediately picked up the new scent, it was different to the other somehow managing to smell sweet yet possess a hint of something that set the fire in my throat burning with the arrival of new blood, I could tell that the scent was masculine by the distinctive smell of testosterone that was prevalent in the scent that the new student had left, I found it strange that a new student had enrolled since there was only a week left of term so I doubt if he would be doing much work for the rest of the week.

I walked to my first class that also followed the trail of the new smell I sniffed again trying to work out what is was in the scent that made it smell so good, I turned the corner and walked towards the door of my class, I turned the handle accompanied by a group of students entering the same class as me, I saw the teacher Mrs Sanera the teacher of History, I sniffed the air in the room, the scent that had seemed so strong in the corridor now filled the room and my throat again began to burn with the urge to feed upon the strange scent, my eyes followed my nose to the source of the scent, my eyes ran quickly over the boy or I suppose man technically who sat in the seat next to mine, he was attractive even by my high standards and I found myself fascinated by his face, he had blonde hair and possessed slightly tanned skin, his eyes scanned over me and I noticed the bright blue eyes that he used to scan over me, I saw how his pupils dilated as he looked over my body and I was intrigued by his face, so smooth as his soft skin swept down across his sharp cheekbones towards his dull red lips, the t-shirt that clung to his chest through which I could see his muscular chest and nipples.

Mrs. Sanera motioned for me to sit interrupting me from my examination of the only person in the room who I found my eyes drawn to, I moved towards the desk and placed my backpack on the desk before sitting down in the chair that was next to the him, I turned my head to face him and saw that he was scanning me as I was him, I saw his eyes trail down my body taking in the muscles that were prominent through the tight material of the t-shirt that clung to my chest, I scanned him too enjoying how I could see his how inviting his arms looked showing through the short sleeves of his t shirt, I quickly scanned the surface of his thoughts using much of my concentration since the sunlight weakened my powers, I sensed that he too was enjoying the way my muscles bulged through my shirt and I was happy to find that his tastes too ran on the more masculine side, I introduced myself first speaking seductively using one of my more basic powers of persuasion all the while scanning the surface of his mind seeing how my words were received.

"Hello, my name is Dominic, I see that you are new here, So what is your name?" his heart sped up as I spoke, and I scanned his mind enjoying how he enjoyed my voice, he spoke and I enjoyed his voice as he spoke slowly "hi I'm Cayden, and you don't sound like you're from America" I listened to his accent and noticed how it was was familiar, I placed it as English and remembered it from my time in England in the 1850's, his teeth glistened as he smiled at me and I felt myself becoming excited by him my dick stirring in my pants.

Cayden is a druid of the ancient supernatural and a tattoo artist and uses vampire blood to create a magical tattoo, to keep a wolf from going rogue. Deep baritone voice with a southern accent, Black, very short hair except for his mohawk. Has multiple piercings including a small hoop in one corner of his lip, He's fun, outgoing, and quite a joyous person, but gets very serious when things get dangerous or serious.

My mind worked at a much faster rate than his so I had plenty of time to formulate my answer, as I was in the middle of my thoughts of my answer I was again distracted by his smile the way his perfect teeth shone in the light flooding through the window next to us.

I answered him after finally pulling my eyes away from his smile and up to his eyes "well you don't exactly sound native either, English correct?" I already knew the answer but it would seem more human if I feigned stupidity, he blinked at me and again smiled before answering "you sound Irish, and yes you are correct I am English".

I could not answer as Mrs. Sanera began the class and started with a question directed at the class, history was of little interest to me and I soon found myself concentrating on the wonderful way that Cayden's lips moved and marveling at the way his voice always seemed to sound seductive, Mrs. Sanera directed a question at me and I pulled the answer from the millions of answers and facts that filled my head, she looked annoyed by my lack of hesitation between her question and my answer.

Cayden too seemed impressed answer and I again found myself mesmerized by his smile before I mistakenly inhaled his scent, the smell was even more wonderful up close his sweetness made my throat ache with the urge to drink from him, but I knew that there were too many witnesses for me to risk a quick snack no matter how tempting the way the skin on his neck looked, the pulse that I could see in the thick vein on his neck was not helping my control.

He noticed how I was staring at him and leaned in close to whisper in my ear, his hot breath sending a tingling sensation across my cheek as he leaned in towards my ear, his skin briefly touched mine and I felt the urge to claim this human as my own his neck was just inches away from my lips and I felt the gums above my canines that housed my fangs itched with the urge to be freed and to sink into the soft seductive flesh of his neck.

He whispered in my ear while I was lost in my thoughts of him, "Dominic, I don't know if you find me attractive but let me tell you that the moment you walked through the door, I wanted to kiss you".

He gently bit my earlobe before he leaned back and I saw that his cheeks were flushed, I too felt the blood run to my cheeks slowly since I had no heartbeat and I saw him a wink as he leaned back into his seat, my mind ranged out touching the minds of all those except Cayden in the room and erasing the past few minutes from their brains.

The class bell rang before I was ready for it to be, and noticed how as soon as Cayden had left his seat, I felt an urge to pull him back and hold him with me here and to kiss him and feed on him, I followed him ignoring my next lesson, he walked through the corridors searching for something before he found the bathroom and I followed him in turning to see him leaning against the nearest wall with a smile on his face.

Even though I had only met him but an hour ago I found myself warming to him in ways I had not thought possible, I moved towards him dropping my backpack on the floor ignoring everything around me except Cayden.

I moved towards him and leaned in towards his face seeing the flush in his cheeks as I got closer, I gently kissed his cheek seeing the flush of heat.

I pulled his arms from his sides and placed them above his head pinning his wrists together with one of my hands, he smiled as I moved closer and moved my face towards his, I leaned in and touched my nose to his jaw bone and ran it along it towards his cheek bone, I felt the muscles contract as his smile grew wider, I ran my cheek against his and felt the heat as his face flushed I looked up and caught his gaze I leaned in using my right hand to secure his wrists above his head and my left to secure his face, my lips gently brushed his and I felt him respond eagerly his lips molding themselves to mine ignoring the slightly colder temperature of my skin, he shivered under my touch as my left thumb caressed his cheekbone, my lungs unresponsive to the lack of oxygen gave me little knowledge of his need for air, he broke away turning his face away unable to back away since his back was against the wall, I ran my lips down his face pressing them against his throat a dangerous move since I was already resisting the urge to rip of his pants and fuck him up the wall, he shivered again and I pressed my body against him, my right hand released his wrists and he eagerly moved them down to the small of my back pulling me closer against him.

I moved my face up unable to resist him anymore and pressed my lips against his once again, his hands grasped against my t-shirt as his muscular arms tried to hold me against him, I breathed in his scent once again lost in the sweetness of his blood, my hand moved down his chest gently squeezing the muscles through his t-shirt, I reached the crotch of his pants and felt his cock already hard through the material and gently squeezed causing him to moan into my mouth, I was so lost with the feeling of his lips against mine that I did not hear the door open, I grew angry at being disturbed, Cayden was mine and now when I had him alone some stupid little fucking human chose to disturb me.

I broke the kiss with Cayden and he who slumped against the wall his eyes closed as he gasped trying to catch his breath, the boy was in a lower year he looked angry though and I could smell rather than see the disgust that mingled with his scent, he squared himself up to me, I laughed and smiled showing my teeth he moved forward and I felt my fangs involuntarily descend elongating my canines, he gasped and moved back into the other wall of the small bathroom, I moved forward grasping his mind with my own, I erased the last ten minutes from his memory and placed a command in his head to leave and act as though nothing had happened.

He left his eyes unfocused, I turned around to see Cayden standing right behind me I leaned in for another kiss and felt his tongue enter my mouth fear filled me as his tongue gently ran up one of my canines, he broke away and looked at my face seeing my fangs which I had forgotten to retract, I reached into his mind seeing his fear, I moved closer taking his face in my hands, he quivered at my touch I did not use my powers as I spoke to him "Cayden please, this is what I am, I know you are scared but, you...you have no idea how long I have lived and you are the only one who had ever been able to make me feel like this".

He shook again before he broke away from my touch I saw him run from the room but I could not move I was locked In a place as I saw him leave, my heart which had been still for 228 years thudded quietly as he left the room, my eyes pricked as a single tear of blood rolled down my face, I had opened myself up and had been stabbed in the heart, I recovered with rage in my heart the boy!!!!!

He had alerted Cayden to what I was, he would suffer for his blunder, I would drain him of his blood slowly watching as the color drained from his face as he slowly fell into death.

I moved slowly through the halls smelling the scent that had belonged to me but five minutes ago, he had left the school and I could smell the trail that his car had left the school grounds, I felt an urge to follow and did not notice as I easily moved fast enough even in the sunlight to reach Cayden' home before he did, I moved towards his house and found that he lived but a few blocks away from my own home, his house was old and I heard no heartbeats on the inside of the house and I moved towards the back of his home and located an old window which I opened easily.

I moved to the front door and listened as Cayden's car approached, he opened his car door and slammed it slowly, I heard the air hitch in his throat as he approached the door the jangle of keys as he unlocked the door, he opened it and closed it behind him he rested his head against the wood and I again heard the air hitch in his throat, my eyes pricked and drop of blood trickled down my cheek, he turned and looked shocked when he saw me, I looked up at him and his lips twitched when he saw me.

I smiled before I spoke "Cayden I know I scare you, but what you do not understand is that I am over 228 years old and in all of that time I have never felt anything like I did for you today, if you do not want me I can understand, if you do not want me I will leave and you will never see me again, no matter how much that will break my heart though it does not beat, if you want me to stay know that I will love you and give you more than any human man could".

He looked down and I closed my eyes and felt another drop of blood roll down my cheek, a soft pair of lips pressed against mine and I jerked a little before realizing that it had to be Cayden, I returned the kiss and wrapped my arms around his muscular frame, he broke the kiss and I stared into his eyes as he leaned forward and with his tongue gently licked away a droplet of blood slightly smeared by our kiss but it was still enough, he gasped.

I knew what he was tasting, the sweetness of my blood, to humans the blood of vampires does not cause them to become like me but even the smallest drop will cause them to become extremely aroused and grant them increased strength and also meant that I would always be able to find him, now no-one will ever take this human away from me, he would be mine soon as would his blood.

Again he pressed his lips against mine the texture warm and soft. For the moment I let him take the dominant role. We both knew I was the stronger but I allowed him to pin me against the closet wall. I ran my hand down his chest feeling the developed muscles tighten against my touch. Lower still my hand went over the rough denim of his jeans until my hand covered his crotch. Squeezing it gently I heard him moan, the noise reverberating in my mouth. Grasping the bottom of my t-shirt he pulled himself away tugging and pulling it over my head to reveal my pale white chest.

My sensitive skin tingled as he ran his fingers over my chest and a loud moan erupted from me when his finger trailed over my right nipple.

Breathing in his heady scent I felt my fangs descend as I lost control.

I froze as I looked at him and so did he for a moment before he leaned in and gently ran his tongue around my lips before gently nipping the skin against my fang, a droplet of his blood touched my tongue and I gasped at the taste so sweet and heady, he smiled as he saw my reaction.

Sniffing the air I could smell his smell and picking him up quickly I followed it to his room. Kicking open the door I noted the single bed in the corner of the room and I dropped him unceremoniously onto it.

Straddling him I ground my ass against his crotch hearing him groan in pleasure.

I leaned down and pressed my lips forcefully against his pushing my tongue past his lips and into the velvet folds of his mouth.

He eagerly accepted me and sucked greedily on my tongue as I reached down to rub his cock through his jeans again, Stopping my assault on his mouth I sat and stared at him before suddenly ripping the shirt from his back.

Underneath his hairless body was lain out before me. It was flawless to look at, well-defined pecs and a washboard flat stomach with a six-pack any guy would be proud of.

It was at that moment that with a huge sense of pride I realized he was mine. No one whether human or vampire could take him away from me. I would die to protect him.

I knew then that he was the one, my mate. My mate? I had never had a mate before but now as I straddled this human I knew that someday I would make him like me but first I would take him to the peak of ecstasy as a human.

"Is something wrong?" His eyes and voice showed his fear. In fact, I could almost smell it mingled in his scent along with the smell of his arousal.

"No Cayden nothing is wrong, I was just thinking of how you are mine"

He smiled and began to pull me down into a kiss with him

Letting my fangs protrude I leaned forward and whispered in his ear,

"Relax this won't hurt much just the initial bite."

Brushing his neck with my fangs I waited silently as he turned it away from me baring it for me. His trust was implicit and nuzzling into his neck I kissed the spot I intended to bite.

I hoped doing it gently would make the bite less painful and has my fangs pierced his skin I heard him gasp before the enzymes in my mouth began to spread pleasure throughout his body dulling the pain of my feeding from him.

His blood tasted so sweet like nothing I had tasted in all my years as a vampire. Not wanting to drink him to the point of death I drank slowly savoring his sweet taste.

I could feel his hand on the back of my neck drawing me closer, holding me to him. His blood tasted so good that I wondered if I would ever get used to the desire that raced through my veins every time he was near me. God, I hoped not.

I broke away hearing him moan in frustration as the source of his pleasure was cut off.

Sitting up I stared down at him and as I stared I trailed an ice-cold finger over his chest, over his nipple, and down further watching as his perfect stomach rippled with my touch.

Leaning forward I followed with my lips where my fingers had just been until I reached the waistband of his jeans.

With practiced ease and an unnatural slowness, only a vampire could know I unbuttoned the button before undoing the zip finally allowing his hard cock freedom from the first layer of its prison. I pulled his jeans off him in one fluid movement before kissing my way back up his legs. The black boxers he wore showed the extent of his arousal.

I kissed his inner thigh and he moaned with pleasure, I reached his boxers and pulled them down as a mad man possessed I had to take him, his cock now free of its cloth prison pointed skyward the skin of his cock was tanned like the rest of his skin with a dark bush of pubes at the base of his it.

I kissed the sensitive head which poked through his foreskin causing him to gasp loudly, His hand on the back of my head running it through my brown hair affectionately was all the encouragement I needed, quick as a flash I took him into my mouth making him scream with pleasure, I went down on his cock and deep throated him easily as I played with his balls with my left hand, he tugged at my hair and thrust his hips upwards to meet my mouth as I sucked without needing to come up for air.

Very gently I let my fangs run along with the head of his cock and felt him shudder and moan loudly, a drop of pre cum formed on his piss slit, I tasted it, god it tasted as good as his blood.

I moved my head faster and faster sucking greedily on his cock waiting for the reward which I knew would soon be mine, he grunted and I felt his balls tighten as he squirmed waiting for the imminent release which he was being brought closer to by my mouth on his cock.

Hearing him gasp loudly and shake beneath me I felt his cock spasm before he shot his load into my waiting mouth, the taste was like nectar.

I had tasted blood from some of the most handsome men in my vampire existence but nothing compared to this.

I knew that it was worth the work that I had done to get it, he moaned and fell back to the bed his arms laying flat at his sides his fists clenched, I continued to suck and soon he was groaning again as his body's refractory period tried to stop him from cumming again, I kept on sucking and he inhaled in both pain and pleasure as his extra-sensitive cock again shot his cum into my eager mouth, he was paralyzed with pleasure and I moved my hand to his cock as he continually spurted volley after volley of cum into the air, I caught each one and swallowed greedily allowing his hot juice to warm my cold body, soon Cayden was moaning and I leaned In close to his face and kissed his cheek, I obliged and looked at his sweaty body and smiled at the fact that this tanned hunk was now mine forever as I leaned down and kissed his tired lips before continuing to beat his cock sending him into a haze in which he experienced both pain and pleasure as I milked his hard cock for every drop that he had, draining him of his fluids and bringing him higher and higher before I allowed him to slip into sleep, I cut one of my fingertips and allowed a few drops of my blood to fall into his open mouth causing his body to replenish itself and restoring the fluids which I had just drained from his body.

He slept for around an hour the sun reaching its height and blazing away through the window, he woke slowly still in my arms him naked and me topless, I kissed his neck and felt his heart quicken as I tightened my grip on him pulling him against my cold frame, he yawned and sat up pulling me with him, turning towards me I saw him lower his face flushing red, I placed one hand on his chin and pulled his face up to mine,

"I feel so safe with you, when you bit me, god it was," he spoke slowly and sleepily.

I cut him off smiling.

"I know, you tasted so sweet, and you are so attractive, I love the feeling of your warmth against my skin"

He smiled, I expected him to shy away from the coolness of my skin but instead, he leaned in closer and pressed his lips against my throat inhaling the smell of my skin, I chuckled as he ran his lips down my throat kissing the skin gently as he moved his lips down my pale skin.

"Cayden if you thought that was good trust me this will make it better" he looked up as I moved my wrist to my mouth and bit into the flesh allowing my blood to flow slowly out from the puncture wounds, he looked up at me surprised before he slowly moved his lips to my wrist and gently began to drink from me, as he drank he moaned around my wrist letting my blood slide down his throat.

I grasped his face with my other hand and pulled him up to my lips, he rolled over and straddled me leaning down to kiss me forcefully.

My hands moved to his back feeling the developed muscles beneath them and marveling at the smoothness of his skin, he broke away suddenly, however, and began to laugh, I looked up at him sitting naked on top of me, I noticed how his breathing was irregular and I sat up pushing him off me and into a sitting position on the edge of his bed.

He turned his head to me smiling widely as he looked into my face.

"So beautiful," I said running the back of my hand over his cheek.

He closed his eyes and leaned against my hand before opening them and asking in a sad tone

"Why me?"

I moved my hand away from his cheek as I answered him shocked at the question.

"What?"

"What is so special about me? What do you, a 228-year-old god-like vampire, see in a human-like me?"

I put my hand under his chin and probed his mind, I saw that I was his first, he had never kissed a man before and that today when he had seen me he had indeed found me attractive but had seen himself as ugly and unworthy of me.

I gasped as I read his mind shocked that he would think I was only going to use him

'You are wrong, you are not ugly to me I find you so very attractive, what first drew me to you was your scent, so sweet and pure but now I have seen what is within your heart you are good and pure and I felt myself falling for you from the moment I laid eyes on you."

He looked up stunned and leaned forward resting his head against my chest, I stroked his hair as I waited for him to calm down, a few minutes later he stood up and I watched him move away from the bed enjoying the way his arse moved, as he walked out of the door, he stopped in the doorway and looked back at me before saying slowly obviously hesitant as to how I would respond "I'm going for a shower maybe..." he trailed off.

Instead, I took the question from the surface of his mind and smiled at his request. When I stood and nodded my agreement he looked shocked. From his wardrobe, he gathered a towel and some white briefs. I moved to his side in the blink of an eye and he smiled shyly before walking out of the door into the hallway.

I followed him slowly. Leaning against the doorway I watched as he turned on the tap of the large shower noting how spacious the room was with its large bathtub as well as the shower.

His heartbeat quickened as he turned and shyly smiled at me

I moved towards the shower and as I got closer he relaxed. As he watched I undid the button on my jeans before moving on to the zipper.

His heartbeat quickened as I revealed the red boxers I was wearing underneath. He gulped when he saw the bulge in them and moved into the shower facing the showerhead immersing himself In the stream of water, the sight of the water running down his firm back to his arse and down his legs made my cock twitch as I removed my boxers letting them fall to the floor.

Stepping into the shower I wrapped my arms around his waist resting my chin on his shoulder and pressing my lips to the hot skin of his throat, the sensitive skin on my lips alerted me to his change in a heartbeat now irregular and quick, Cayden turned around and faced me resting his arms on my shoulders, he looked at my body and gasped when he had scanned me, his eyes lingered over my cock and I pulled him closer bringing our cocks into contact with each other, I spoke seductively to him

"Do you like what you see?" he blinked at me before responding.

"So beautiful" I chuckled and pulled his face up to mine pressing my lips to his, his heartbeat tripled and I felt his cock swelled against mine as his fingers knotted in my hair holding me against his warm body.

He bared his throat to me obviously expecting me to bite, I let my fangs descend and moved them over my previous bite wound before gently kissing the spot and pulling away, he moaned in annoyance that I was not going to bite him, but what he did not know was that the enzymes that were on my fangs to cause pleasure I could release through almost any other part of my body, from my tongue to my fingers and many other places, I lightly ran my fingers over the pulse in his neck releasing enzymes through my fingertips which were quickly absorbed through the skin into his bloodstream, he moaned as he realized what I was doing, I felt his cock harden against my leg and my own began to stir as he stroked my back the sensitive skin tingling due to his touch.

I felt him use his muscles to push me away, he ran his hand down my chest and down towards my cock, groaning as his fingers stroked my cock gently rubbing the sensitive head, I growled as he wrapped his hand around it squeezing it gently, he smiled pleased by my response, slowly wanking me off.

Thrusting against his hand I growled.

He moved onto his knees and I looked down at him, my eyes glowing with a feral light. The second his lips touched it I moaned loudly and he began to suck on the head, he continued to suck my cock, moving further and further down it gradually taking all of its lengths down his throat.

He gently sucked on my cock driving me higher and higher until I could take it no longer shooting my load into his willing mouth.

Has he stood up he smiled at me and pulling his face closer to mine I tasted my own sweetness on his lips.

I pressed his body back under the stream of water until his back was against the wall of the shower. Crushing his body against the wall with my own, I forcefully pressed my lips against his prising them open and invading his mouth exploring it with my tongue.

He clutched my face to his accepting me eagerly, I ran my hands down his back to his arse clutching the hot flesh pulling his body upwards towards me, I moved my left hand to his thigh pulling it up over him pinning him against my body.

My cock began to rise again pressing against the inside of his thigh, his lips broke away from mine as he nuzzled my neck gently nipping the skin with his teeth, I moved my fangs to his neck before biting the flesh feeling his hot blood flow into my mouth, he tensed at the sudden bite to his neck. His teeth dug into my neck and my blood spilled into his mouth, he tensed again before he began to slowly sip, drawing the blood out through the bite wound moaning at the taste.

We continued to drink from each other replenishing each other as we drank, my blood was more potent than his and caused his body to heat up and his cock to harden against my chest, I broke away, his blood staining my teeth, pushing him away from my neck I heard the moan as he licked the blood from his teeth smiling as he looked up at me with seemingly innocent eyes.

That was before he tensed and used the strength that my blood gave him to push me out of the shower and onto the carpeted floor, he tried to land on me and I knew what he wanted but I would prefer to do it in the comfort of my own home rather than here where Cayden' parents could come home at any moment, he tried to dive on me but I moved too fast and he simply collided with the carpet, I could see the lust in his eyes, I leaned down and whispered in his ear.

"If you want more I think we should take this to a more private location such as my home" he immediately leaped up and wrapped his arms around my waist and pressed his face against my chest.

Disentangling myself from him I moved quickly back into his room dressing without my underwear and returning with an outfit I thought would look good on Cayden, something that would reveal the muscles that bulged out of his chest, I returned with barely a second has passed. Cayden saw the bundle of clothes and eagerly grabbed them putting them on in a rush eager to leave with me.

We walked quickly down the stairs and I put my arm around his waist as we walked through the streets to my home a few blocks away, we walked up the drive to my house and I opened the door quickly with my keys which I pulled from my pocket.

He eagerly walked through the door striding into the spacious front room, I took his hand and pushed him up against the nearest wall gently.

I caressed his face with my hand gently placing my thumb over his lips that parted as I touched them, I kissed him gently, softly but this was not what he wanted, he moaned into my mouth and tugged me closer against him.

I responded forcefully as I was sure he wanted and clutched at him tearing his shirt again, I chuckled slightly as I felt his chest, running my fingertips over his nipples and carefully releasing a small number of pleasure enzymes into the skin, he moaned repeatedly as I ran my hands down his chest feeling his heartbeat quicken once more, my cock began to stir behind my jeans as I was sure he was.

I picked him up and ran quickly to my room before dumping him onto my bed and diving on top of him pinning his hot body beneath me.

He squirmed under my grasp but I silenced his fears with my lips, I felt him relax immediately and I pulled him up onto the large pillows.

I moved my hands to the headboard smiling as I knew he had obviously not seen the chains that dangled behind the headboard, I pulled them over the headboard and pushed his hands together before using my superior speed to quickly wrap his arms together with the cold metal chains, he tugged against them for a second before giving up with a sigh.

I ran my hand down his chest gently massaging the muscles that bulged out from him, he wriggled under my touch but relaxed as soon as I released a small number of pleasure enzymes through his skin.

I ran my fingers down his chest gently stroking his six-pack, I undid the button of his jeans and undid the zip pulling the thin layer of clothing down past his knees, his cock swelled within his boxers, I squeezed his cock through his boxers it twitched under my hand as it swelled to its full size tenting proudly 7" away from his body.

I slowly stroked him, from his face to his nipples which I played with for a while causing him to tug against the chains that bound him to the bed, I reached his boxers and played with the waistband for a while causing him to wriggle in anticipation, he spoke in a low growl "just get on with it already, give me what I want".

I obliged and pulled down his boxers slowly, his cock sprung up free from its cloth prison rising to meet my hand, I ran one of my fingertips up from his balls to the sensitive head, I rubbed slowly over the piss slit causing him a pleasant amount of pain, he moaned loudly thrusting his hips upwards towards my hands.

My ears picked up the sound of feet on the front porch, and heard the sound of my front door opening and tensed immediately, Cayden noticed my sudden freeze and opened his mouth to speak probably to ask what was going on.

I put my hand over his mouth and put my index finger over my lips, he relaxed quickly, I moved to pull his boxers up his legs and doing up his jeans with difficulty over his swollen cock, I undid the chains from around his arms and quickly handed him a t-shirt which I fetched from the nearest drawer.

I tugged on his hand and led him slowly from the room me crouched defensively in front of my mate, I put my hand on his chest when we reached the upstairs hall, he halted, I heard movement downstairs and I kissed him quickly on the lips before jumping off the edge of the balcony down to the ground floor beneath a growl in my throat as I turned to see the intruder, I moved to the living room and looked around and there on the couch sat my....my maker.

I stiffened when I saw him, freezing on the spot as he turned to face his progeny a smile on his lips, I looked into his eyes and listened to him speak as he moved closer to me, "my progeny how good it is to see you, I can tell by the look on your face that you believed that I died in London during the blitz, but that my progeny was necessary at the time, but now I need your help in a matter" Marcus sniffed the air before looking at me and saying "what is that scent?" he looked at me before turning when he heard Cayden' voice from behind me "that would be me and who the fuck are you, we were busy before you came in, so who are you and what do you want?" he moved to my side, I moved in front of him defensively before looking forward at my maker, he looked at Cayden then turned his eyes to me he spoke to me completely ignoring Cayden "I see you have a meal how thoughtful" he took a step toward trying to side step me I snarled at my maker putting my arm in front of Cayden blocking my makers path to him, I snarled at him threateningly "he is my mate and you will not touch him!, I do not care if you are my maker but Cayden is mine!".

He raised his hands in innocence I straightened out of my crouch before looking over at Cayden smiling assuredly at him, he smiled back weakly, I turned to my maker who now was observing Cayden with fascinated eyes, he winked at him before addressing him "to answer your question Cayden, I am Dominic' maker, I am over 486 years old I was made in 1526 by a Spanish vampire in the newly founded city of Santa Marta.

I made Dominic in 1784 after I found him dying in a gutter in Dublin and the reason why I want him is that involving a broken law" he caught my eye and I knew exactly what he meant, someone had found out about us and had to be eliminated quickly before It was made public and our very way of life was challenged.

CHAPTER 2

Marcus moved to the front door opening it quickly and ushering in a woman, she looked around 19 with dark brown hair and sea-green eyes, her eyes quickly scanned over me and Cayden before she retreated behind Marcus clinging onto his arm.

He looked at me before saying "now Dominic we both have something in common, this is Maria, she is my mate and like your Cayden, she is also human".

She looked up and smiled at Cayden before turning her eyes to me with a look of fear in them, Marcus spoke again "now my sweet why don't you go with Cayden over there and find something to eat I have some business to discuss with Lois".

Cayden shot me a glance as Maria moved towards him, he smiled at her before glancing anxiously back at me.

He moved away from me following Maria but not before placing a quick peck on my lips that left me craving more God he knew how to turn me on.

I turned my attention to Marcus who was leading the way out out of the front door, the sun was beginning to set and I felt my full powers begin to manifest as the sun dampening effect lessened my maker spoke to me slowly as soon as the door was closed behind me.

"I see you too have found a mate, have you claimed him yet?"

I shook my head, by claiming he meant having sex with me, I chuckled and said "I was going to soon but you interrupted me, I had him chained to the bed naked before you walked in" he laughed a short laugh before waving his hand dropping the subject.

"When I first smelt him there was something there, he smelled so desirable, the only example of sweetness in the blood is that he is a supernatural, just a little food for thought about your mate.

But now that the sun has almost set I believe we should continue this conversation telepathically don't you think?" I nodded dropping the guards around my mind entering the mind of my maker and absorbing the thoughts closest to the surface.

I saw a young man relatively attractive with black hair and hazel eyes, I saw a vampire chained to a table the blood being drained slowly from his body keeping him weak enough that he was unable to break the chains that had him spread-eagled on the table naked.

The human moved around the table examining the anatomy of the vampire, I broke apart from his mind eager to tear this human to shreds but torn between my need for Cayden and the outrage of this human.

Cayden' Point of View*********

I moved away from Dominic following the woman called Maria into the kitchen away from my mate but not before giving him a quick peck on the lips seeing the look of lust that crossed his face as I moved away following Maria into the kitchen.

I heard the front door open and close, I knew that I would have to go home soon and explain why I missed the whole day of school, I hoped that Dominic would help persuade my Mum, I knew just how persuasive my...boyfriend? No that wasn't what Dominic had called me he had called me his...mate, the very thought of that pale hunk of gorgeousness being mine made me want him in my arms right now.

I wondered if this Maria woman felt the same about her Mate?

The dark-haired one who had interrupted Dominic just as I was about to be truly his.

The woman moved into the kitchen uncertainly as did I, the kitchen was large with a refrigerator in the corner that hummed quietly and a microwave on the counter, there was a cooker against the wall spotless just a prop.

I moved towards the fridge and opened it before slamming it shut just as quickly, all I saw in the fridge were bags of blood stacked on top of each other.

I moved towards the cupboards and found a loaf of bread and some eggs probably for when he had humans here which I guess was not very often.

I began to whisk the eggs before dipping the bread in it and quickly frying it in hot oil, the woman Maria moved to my side watching me cook, I finished cooking the food and plated up the 2 slices of bread that I had cooked.

I ate quickly eager to be rid of these people and to be alone with my mate, the woman Maria began to speak with a Spanish accent and I guessed Marcus that was her mate's name had picked her up when he was in Spain or South America or somewhere.

She spoke slowly in only slightly accented English "so I see you too have found yourself a vampire as a mate, it is wonderful is it not" "yes" I spoke quickly she nodded before asking another question "has he...claimed you yet?"

I shook my head guessing the meaning of her question "I almost was, but you interrupted us"

I said she blushed to mutter a quick apology, she spoke slowly again obviously nervous as to my answer "has..has he bitten you yet?" I nodded smiling, she spoke quickly obviously excited "he has? Marcus has not yet done that to me, what was it like? Did it hurt?" I shook my head answering "the initial bite hurts but after that it is just pure pleasure it was so amazing feeling my strength flowing from me and into him, especially when I bit him and drank from him, God it made me so horny" I spoke quickly excited.

She gawked at me, obviously, she had not tasted her vampire yet, my face flushed and I looked down embarrassed, I did not hear the front door open and close, my face was pulled up against my consent, I tensed as I felt a set of lips press against mine but relaxed as soon as I saw that those lips belonged to Dominic, he pulled me up onto my feet and I wrapped my arms around his neck completely ignoring Maria she was lost in the past all that mattered now was holding Dominic here and kissing him.

He pushed his tongue past my lips and I pressed myself closer against his cold body enjoying the way it controlled my rising body heat, my heart began to beat faster and faster as I realized I had forgotten to breathe I didn't care and hardly noticed as my vision began to darken until I fell away from Dominic' lips.

He caught me in his strong arms and pulled me up to his lips again gently breathing into my open mouth, whatever was in his breath began to clear my head and my eyes shot open and I felt a sudden buzz of energy course through me.

Maria was nowhere to be seen but I could not give a fuck all I cared about was Dominic who was easily within arms reach, both his blood and his breath in my system must have done something to my muscles since I moved too quickly towards him surprising him as I threw him onto the floor growling as I felt an uncontrollable urge to dive on top of him and take him inside of me or at least give him the pleasure I so greatly wanted to give to him.

I landed on him pressing my lips once more against his, this time it was me in control and I had this vampire all to myself, I broke away and kissed up the left side of his pale face before once again locking my lips against his, I felt his fangs descend against my tongue gently nipping the skin.

He flipped me over and I bared my throat for him, the angle at which my neck was at must not have been enough for him because he grabbed my jaw bone and pulled my head even further to the side, and dug his fangs into my neck.

The sharp pain made me gasp involuntarily but that was before the enzymes on his fangs went to work in my body, after it had taken effect he could have hacked off a limb I wouldn't have cared, he pulled away and leaned forward to kiss me, I tasted my own blood in his mouth and enjoyed the salty sweetness of it.

He pulled away "I have to leave but don't worry not for long a few hours at most, I will go after you fall asleep," he said barely pulling his lips off of mine.

I grimaced at the thought of him leaving but I realized that he would not be gone long and I would not notice it, I might as well have what I wanted at the moment though even if he would not claim me we could both give each other pleasure.

I pushed forward and rubbed my groin against him, he smiled against my lips before kissing his way up my face.

His throat was directly above my mouth and I leaned forward and pressed my lips against his throat moving to the side of his neck nuzzling the flesh, he knew what I meant to do and I saw the muscles in his neck relax against my mouth, I bit into the flesh enjoying not only the taste of his blood but also the slight chuckle that I heard from him, I sucked weakly on his neck drawing in his blood.

My lips moved off of his neck, I swallowed the blood that was inside my mouth pulling his face down to mine he smiled at me before pressing his lips onto mine, his tongue moved around the inside of my mouth, I sucked greedily on his tongue, my hands moved to his back my nails digging into the smooth flesh beneath his t-shirt, I felt his cool blood on my fingertips, if he felt any pain he didn't complain in fact he showed more passion as he crushed my body beneath his growling into my mouth.

I broke away from his mouth gasping for breath, being around Dominic made all of my normal instincts vanish, he moved his lips down my face to my neck licking the skin over his previous bite wound.

I waited for him to bite me again but instead, he moved his face down my neck to the collar of my t-shirt, his hands moved to the top of my t-shirt tearing the fabric straight down the middle exposing my chest, I chuckled that was 2 of t-shirts he had ripped today, I couldn't care, all I care about was the feeling of his lips moving down my chest, he had reached my nipples and his soft skin felt wonderful against mine, pleasure shot up my body.

He began to move down my body reaching my six-pack he gently kissed each of the muscles before moving his hand towards my crotch, he was completely in control of me, he squeezed my growing cock gently through my jeans, I moaned under his touch thrusting my hips upward into his hand seeking greater friction against it.

He undid the top button of my jeans quickly undoing the zip and yanking them down to my ankles, my cock tented upwards free the first of its prisons, he moved up my leg gently kissing the skin, he reached my left thigh and kissed the skin, pleasure shot up my body again, he moved to my right and I moaned in pleasure, his fingertips trailed up my leg starting at the soles of my feet, he gently stroked the skin his cold fingers sending shivers up my body.

He moved to my chest and his fingers lingered over my nipples before he moved to my face cradling it in his hand, I smiled down at him my fingers weaved into his hair and I tugged him upwards towards my face, now it was his turn.

I rolled onto my side laying him down next to me I ran my hands over his t-shirt feeling his developed muscles beneath the thin layer of cloth, I tugged the bottom of the t-shirt pulling it upward to his head, he sat up and I pulled it over his head.

I stared at his topless form gawking at his perfectly defined muscles and smooth perfect skin, I moved my right hand to his chest placing it over his heart, there was no beat beneath my fingers, he moved the back of his hand against my cheek, and spoke seductively "it may not beat but it feels for you, I do not have long around an hour but in that time we can still have some fun" he smiled cheekily, he stood up in a flash his hand offered to me, I grasped it pulling myself up smiling at him, he picked me up cradling me in his arms in a second we were in his room.

I spoke shocked "I don't think I have fully measured your abilities" he smiled at me again before answering "now that the sun has fully set my powers are at their strongest.

He moved onto the bed and lowered me onto it and then himself onto me.

I felt his legs against mine and realized that he had removed his jeans, his hands ran down my body and he yanked my boxers off, he moved his hands to my cock now semi-hard and stroked the skin lightly, I gasped at his touch my cock and immediately shot upright in his hands, he slowly began to wank my cock.

He sped up and I groaned loudly as he sped up, he replaced his hand quickly with his mouth, he sucked my cock greedily obviously enjoying himself as I moaned under his touch.

I climbed higher and higher I knew that my orgasm was imminent and I was sure that he knew too, he pulled his head away looking up at me smiling widely, he lay down on the bed next to me and I knew exactly what he wanted me to do, I moved my hand towards his 8" cock marveling at it.

I wrapped my fingers around it and slowly began to wank his cock enjoying his reaction to my touch, I sped up as he had noticing how even though he did not need the air his breathing still sped up.

I moved my hand away from his cock noticing the low growl that emanated from his chest I replaced my hand with my mouth and licked the head teasingly, I moved my lips down his cock until my nose reached the base and rested in the dark pubes that surrounded his cock.

The tip of his cock had entered my throat and he growled louder than he had before and I knew that he was getting closer and closer to orgasm, I had tasted him once before and now I wanted to do to him what he had originally done to me, I would suck him until he begged for me to stop.

I felt him shudder against my body and I sucked harder and faster until he howled loudly as he shot into my mouth, I pulled back allowing his second load to land on my tongue, his load tasted sweet and bitter at the same time I swallowed his cum and I continued to suck causing him to shoot again and again into my mouth, I pulled away and wanked his cock as he kept on shooting his load.

Eventually, I collapsed on top of him, he was breathing heavily and had his eyes closed, I lay on top of him and nuzzled myself against his chest, his arms moved from his sides and wrapped around me pulling him against me.

My still hard cock pressed against him and he smiled with his eyes still shut, he moved his hand towards my chest and stroked my abs before moving down to my cock, his cool hands stroked the skin softly, sensually as I slowly got higher and higher, I had been on the verge of cumming when he had pulled away and now I was close, he began to speed up and I shut my eyes as the pleasure built and built until finally, I spurted onto his chest.

I collapsed against his chest kissing the skin of his pecs, his hands moved to my hair and he gently stroked it lovingly as I slipped into a satisfying sleep in the arms of my dark angel.

I woke up slowly reaching out and searching for my Dominic. My fingers clutched at the space next to me in the bed and found nothing. I sat up quickly and looked for him and my heart sank when I saw that his spot next to me on the bed was empty. Then I took notice of the room around me and I realized that I was in my room at home. I looked under the covers and saw that I was still naked from my night with Dominic.

I closed my eyes and tried to remember arriving at my house, but decided Dominic must have carried me home while I was sleeping. I remembered the night before and my cock hardened as I remembered the feel of Dominic' skin against mine and his hands all over my body. I closed my eyes and ran my hand over my abs down towards my hardening cock. When I reached it and gently ran my fingers up its shaft, my skin tingled as I envisioned Dominic' doing it. I could almost feel him next to me. It wasn't until I opened my eyes that I realized Dominic was next to me now.

My hands flew towards him and I pulled him onto me crushed my lips against his. I pushed my tongue against his lips, seeking entrance, but I broke away when his hand wrapped around my cock and a moan escaped from my lips as he slowly began to wank me. I not only felt his hand on my cock but I could feel what he felt and I knew exactly how much he wanted me and just how good I smelled to him. I moaned loudly, with the sensations from his touch too, I quickly came on his hand.

He must have sensed something was wrong and entered my head because I heard him gasp and my eyes locked with his as he began to speak, "Cayden, I think I know why you smell so good. And not just to me. Marcus said something about your scent too. I didn't realize it at first, but now it all makes sense. You smell so good and taste even better because of what I think is magic in your blood. Marcus suggested that you weren't completely human. I am guessing you never experienced anything like what just happened, right? It seems you experienced empathy with touch. That is why you knew how I was feeling just now. There are other powers too, I am guessing."

I looked at him dumbfounded before I silently whispered, "How?"

He gulped before saying, "Magic is normally only unlocked during times of extreme danger, but I am guessing that my blood jump-started it." I thought quickly my thoughts racing. "So what does this mean? What do I do now?"

He smiled at me before pulling himself off the bed and answering me while pulling up a pair of shorts. "Now that your powers are active they will begin to get stronger, so why not try it now? Focus on something and say whatever comes into your head."

My eyes flickered around the room finding only one thing in my head. I wanted Dominic now. I looked at him concentrating saying, "Dominic, come over here." My voice sounded lower and was layered with different voices as his shorts flew down his legs and he was dragged back onto the bed. He landed on his back and I saw the look of shock on his face which I quickly silenced with a touch of my lips. I kissed his lips before moving down to his collar bone running my nose along with it before proceeding lower onto the tight muscles of his pecs, I kissed around his nipples before running my tongue around it gently sucking it into my mouth, I heard him moan in pleasure as I sucked.

I began to move lower kissing his well-defined six-pack before reaching his cock. He was hard and I ran my hand up his thigh to gently cup his balls. He moaned under my touch and I began trailing kisses up his thigh towards his now hard dick, I took him into my mouth and ran my tongue over the sensitive head of his dick marveling at its taste and enjoying the way his hands clutched at my hair pulling me further down his shaft. I sucked hard on his dick bobbing my head up and down on it, I squeezed his balls gently and felt them pull closer to his body. I replaced my mouth with my hand and again tried to force him with my newfound magic. "Cum for me, Dominic, and let me taste you," I said as his eyes rolled back into his head. I felt his balls tighten again and I quickly locked my mouth over the head of his dick waiting for him to release into my mouth.

Dominic came in an explosion that filled my mouth and began to dribble down my chin, I half-swallowed keeping some of his cum in my mouth and moved up to his lips and pressed against them pushing into his mouth, letting him taste his own cum. I pulled away and he spoke in a dazed voice, "God, that was the best I've ever...ever had! Your magic is strong and you are even able to control a vampire over 200 years old. You have to be a descendant of one of the witches from either the Hakara coven from Ireland or the Danaro coven from London. I am guessing the latter."

Dominic continued, "I'm sorry I didn't see you when I finished helping Marcus last night. You were fast asleep and I didn't want to wake you, so I brought you home. Now we have to get to school so we don't bring any more attention to ourselves. I believe the plans Marcus had made for tonight were interrupted, so we could go somewhere if you would like?"

I nodded quickly, wanting any opportunity to be with Dominic. He grinned after I nodded Dominic said, "Try not to kill anyone with your new powers. He said that with a stern look on his face and then grinned, "But, seriously, try not to lose your temper with anyone when you are angry or scared because you will instinctively try to defend yourself." I have erased the memory of the teachers so only the pupils will realize that you were missing yesterday. Today, try to take care of that sexy ass. I want it in one piece when I come home for it." Dominic smiled and lent forward to press his lips against mine and my heart began to beat faster as his tongue pushed past my lips and into my mouth. He pulled away too soon and I sighed as he pulled away. I opened my eyes and stared into his as he leaned in again and gave me a quick peck on the lips leaving me lusting for more. I groaned as he moved away, once again, to get dressed. I moaned before saying, "Do I have to drag you back here, using magic, for another kiss?"

He had just pulled up his underwear and he turned around with a lusty glint in his eye. He dived on top of me and pinned my arms above my head and growled at me before saying lustily, "You have no idea how much I want to take you right now, not just your body, but your blood as well." His fangs descended and I pushed my head up against his chest kissing the cool flesh causing him to growl deeply before ramming his mouth against mine. His tongue delved into my mouth forcing mine into submission.

I moaned around his lips before he pulled away staring into my eyes again. I spoke to him, clearly making my words an order, "Bite me."

Dominic grinned before saying, "All you had to do was ask," and he pressed his lips against my throat not biting but gently nipping the skin drawing a small amount of blood. I growled before saying with a growl in my voice, "Don't fucking tease me, just bite me." He quickly bit into my skin, drawing the blood out of my body in quick gulps and I felt his body grow warm against mine as he drew the blood out of my neck.

The pain of the initial bite had already faded and was replaced by a feeling of euphoria that spread from the venom in Dominic' fangs. He continued to drink from me and pulled away before I was ready, he looked down at my face and smiled knowingly, then he brought his wrist up to his lips and bit down tearing the soft flesh, his eyes never leaving mine. He placed it against my lips and allowed the blood to trickle into my mouth. My hands moved weakly to his wrist, holding it gently against my lips. His blood tasted sweet on my tongue and I drank from him replenishing my supply of blood with his. He pulled his wrist away from my mouth, smiling lovingly at me. His fangs sparkled in the light that was shining through my window and he moaned as he rolled his body off of mine, saying regretfully, "You have no idea how much I want to take you, to be inside of you but...."

I looked at him and drew in an audible breath when I saw the look of complete love in his eyes. "Dominic, I trust you, I want you to take me and I know you won't hurt me. God, I've known you for only a day, and yet I feel myself already...in... love with you."

"Cayden, I don't just mean physically, though I will have to work hard to control myself since I am so much stronger than you. If you want me, all you have to do is ask, but know that once I have taken you, we will belong to each other. I to you and you to me, We will be one after that and it would destroy the other if one were to die. But being one also means nothing could ever separate us and no matter the distance, we will always be able to find each other."

I looked at him, I knew that he had to go, but it was not until we heard my mum coming up the stairs that he vanished in a streaking blur out of my window. I quickly pulled on a pair of white briefs before my mum walked in and told me that breakfast was on the table. "Mum! Can't you knock?"

She turned to leave while saying, "Breakfast is ready and if you were ready like you should be, it wouldn't have been a problem." I quickly put on a pair of blue jeans and another white t-shirt, making a note in my head to get more of them. I was envisioning later on when Dominic would rip my t-shirt off again as I moved down the stairs, still deep in thought. I heard a slight rush of wind, then felt a gentle brush of pressure against my lips before it was gone. I stopped, shocked, then I heard the familiar chuckle of Dominic as I headed down the stairs. He was teasing me and, God, he knew how to do that soooooo easily.

I entered the kitchen and saw that my Mum had cooked me a full English breakfast. I sat down and began to eat slowly and my mum sat down at the table and started to talk to me, "So how was your first day at school?"

I shrugged my shoulders at her and she smiled and continued, "So did you meet anyone nice?" I blushed and looked down and she leaned in interested and said, "So?"

I nodded and smiled and said, "Yes, I met someone nice."

She smiled again and said, "So who is she?"

"He, it is a he, not a she and yes, he is really nice."

A look of shock crossed her face. "Oh," was all that came out of her mouth before I heard the slight chuckle from somewhere in the house that made my heart freeze.

My mother also heard it and froze as well. I heard the front door open and close before Dominic sauntered into the kitchen with a smug grin on his face. My mother took one look at him before jumping to her feet and backing into the wall.

Dominic looked surprised by her reaction but held up his hands in surrender. My mother's index and middle fingers had already come together and she pointed them at Cayden as she chanted, "Ic bebindan aet se mur!" "She swung her arm towards the nearest wall and Dominic was thrown against it with his arms pinned to his side.

I stood there unmoving and shocked! My mom had magic too? Did she know that I did? I was so stunned I didn't say anything.

My Mum had a look of anger on her face as she spoke to Dominic again, chanting a spell, "Bodian se so^sagu!" She continued "Now vampire, why are you here and what do you want?"

A look of horror crossed Dominic' face as his lips began to move, "I brought Cayden home last night and all I want is...him." The last word was clearly pulled from him as if he didn't want to say it. He cast his eyes down in shame, my mum moved backward slightly, but her hand remained where it was holding him against the wall.

I stopped all the questions running through my head and finally said something, "Mum, put him down, now!" My voice remained steady but I was holding back the urge to hit something. She looked at me with a surprised look on her face before she nodded and muttered something in the same language she had used to bind him to the wall.

He moved away from the wall before he looked at me and gave me a quick smile before turning back to my mum, "I see that the magic runs in your blood as well. Know this, Cayden is safe with me and the last spell you cast proved that. You know that is true because if my knowledge of the language you used is correct, then it was a truth spell. So for now, I cannot lie. I can assure you that I cannot and will not ever harm him."

My mum relaxed when she heard this and her shoulders slumped. She turned to me and said, "So this is the guy you were telling me about, Cayden? He is not just another boy. Just promise me something..."

I looked at her and said, "I know what he is, mum. I'm more interested in finding out what and who I am."

Her eyes turned soft as she looked at me and said, "Keep safe, my son, And you, blod drincere, know that I may not be as powerful as my son is, but know that I still have enough magic in this body to tear your limbs off one by one with ease. So, you better keep your word and not harm my son in any way." She turned back to me and said, "I know I owe you some explanations. I can feel your magic now. Be careful until you learn how to use it. They are still growing and you are already more powerful than me. That is because of your father. We both came from families with strong magic it was forbidden for us to be together since any child we had would possess great power. But, your father was more powerful than I am. He was from the Danaro coven and when he...died, he knew that he would live on in you. I am from the Hakara coven. Now enough magic talk for now. We will talk more, later. Now, off to school, both of you, before I fling you out kicking and screaming."

She shot a glance at Dominic, who was smiling, before leading us to the front door and handing me my backpack. She waved goodbye as I walked out of the door. Dominic followed close behind me towards his car parked in the driveway. When we reached his car he pulled me into his arms and I snuggled into his chest enjoying the coolness of his skin, I tilted my head upwards and kissed up his neck towards his mouth.

He froze and said, "Your mum is watching."

I reached his jaw and muttered, "So?" He smiled before he gingerly pressed his lips against mine, his tongue gently circled my lips, then pulled away chuckling when he saw the look on my face. I got into his car and he sat down beside me starting the engine and pulling slowly out of the driveway of my house. My eyes never left his face as he drove to school and my thoughts visualized the night before and the night ahead.

We arrived at school and I got out nervously until Dominic offered me his hand. I clutched at it and he pulled me towards him with his back against the car not caring about the other people in the parking lot, of which there weren't many. He leaned closer to kiss me and the moment his lips touched mine, I couldn't care about the other people in the lot either and my hands ran up his chest clutching at the thin material of his shirt. Firm hands pushed me away from him and I gasped for air as I leaned back against the car for support next to Dominic. His hand reached up to my face and he gently ran his fingertips down it. I looked down as my face blushed and he smiled and pressed his forehead against mine, I noticed how his eyes had slightly darkened and said softly, "You are so cute when your blushing, it...makes me hungry, the thin membrane of your cheeks reveals the sweet blood that hides beneath."

I looked up at him and saw his green eyes glisten slightly as he stared at me. "So beautiful," he said, and I flipped us around so that it was him who had his back against the car. He smiled again and I leaned forward and gave him a quick peck on the lips before turning away from him and walking towards the main school. He followed and ended up next to me in an instant. He turned his head to me and said, "You can be such a tease when you want to be, I'm finding it hard to control myself."

I led the way to the school and turned my head towards him and said, "If you want some come to get it." I ran flat out toward the school away from him, I reached the doorway a few seconds later and walked into a deserted hallway, breathing heavily with my back against the door. The school seemed deserted, I closed my eyes and waited for the door to open and for Dominic to walk in. I should've known he would reach the school before me. A set of lips pressed against my throat and I felt two hands pin me against the door. I moaned under the touch knowing that it was Dominic, his lips moved up and down my throat teasing my flesh with his lips.

I gasped quietly, "Not here, should we...should we...take this to the location of our first kiss?" I opened my eyes to find his level with mine and he nodded and pulled up my hand tugging me forward towards the bathroom.

Time seemed to slow down the closer we got to the bathroom and when we finally arrived in what felt like no more than a second flat, I was pinned against the wall with my hands above my head. Dominic' lips once again found mine, his tongue pressed gently against my lips, I accepted him and our tongues slid over each other. I moaned into his mouth and was rewarded with a growl that emanated from his chest and I was happy that I could cause him to become so turned on by just a simple kiss.

Dominic released my hands and I moved them to his face and pulled him closer to me as he ran his hands down my chest. I knew where his hands were going and I pressed into his body. His hand reached my rock-hard dick and he squeezed me gently causing my lips to break away from his as I moaned loudly against his neck. He whispered into my ear, his cool breath creating a tingling sensation against my skin, "We're going to be late if we don't stop messing around...now."

I panted against his neck. He continued to stroke me through my trousers and growled, "Do you want to stop?"

I answered breathlessly, "You know I don't," as he ran his nose up my neck.

He inhaled deeply and said, "You smell so good, can I... just have a quick snack to hold me over till later?"

"Only if you return the favor," he smiled at me as his canines lengthened.

I leaned forward and ran my tongue up one of his fangs, feeling the sharp point run along with my tongue. My hands were still holding his face and I pulled him towards my neck as I leaned in towards his. Our bodies were pressed together and both of our cocks were rock hard. He ran his fangs along the vein in my neck and my heart began to beat faster as he positioned his fangs over my skin. I made the first move and bit down into the cool skin of his neck, his sweet blood filled my mouth and I quickly swallowed. I reveled in the taste of his blood. It was so sweet and seemed to enhance all of my feelings. The taste of Dominic' blood seemed to get stronger as did the softness of his skin against my hands.

His fangs ferally broke through the skin of my neck. Momentary pain shot up my neck before being replaced with pure pleasure. I swallowed a few more mouthfuls of his blood before breaking away. He continued to drink from my neck for a few moments longer before he too pulled away from my flesh. He pulled one of his fingers up to his mouth and gently pricked the flesh before rubbing the blood against the bite marks on my neck, the skin tingled and I knew he was healing bite wounds that he had left. I stilled his hand and leaned forward to lick a drop that had begun to run down his neck from the unsealed wound. I felt him shiver. I then kissed the spot and stood back while the skin of the wounds began to knit, healing the marks.

I looked up and met his eyes knowing that if the need I saw on his face and felt in my own body was anything to go by, tonight would be…

We walked out of the bathroom together our hands intertwined. I clung to his side as we walked to our biology class with someone called Mr. Bidle. Dominic walked confidently through the school always remaining no further than a foot away from me. His presence seemed to have an effect on, not just me, but on both the guys and the girls. The guys looked at him with jealousy and the girls looked at him with only lust.

Dominic slowed as we reached a classroom door, he leaned in close to my ear and whispered, "Ignore those stupid cattle. They follow the herd and all it takes is a new male to stir them into a frenzy. All I ask is that you try not to get angry. I would hate to see one of them hurt." The sarcasm was evident in his voice and I tried to focus as we walked through the door.

I sensed their glares, digging into my back as we walked in. As we looked for a seat, I fervently hoped Dominic and I could sit together. I saw a girl stand up from the two-person desk and move to another in the back of the room. Dominic and I walked over and sat at the empty desk and he put his hand on my knee after we were seated. I couldn't help but wonder if she had moved of her own free will.

"Don't think about trying to use your powers focus on something else like me...naked".

I thought it was stupid but I did it anyway. Dominic' hand gently running up and down my leg did not help my concentration, but I knew I wouldn't be able to calm down while I could feel people looking at me and feel their jealousy. I suddenly noticed something. A buzz seemed to flow through me and my mind flew as I found that some sort of language seemed to have been unlocked inside my head. And crazier yet, I seemed to understand it.

Suddenly, my eyes shot open and I felt as if I had been lying down for an hour and suddenly gotten up. Blood rushed to my head and white spots appeared in front of my eyes. I would have hit the desk if Dominic hadn't put a hand on my shoulder to steady me. He said quietly, "It seems that you have discovered your second language. From my basic translation, I believe you said, 'Hide me from those who are jealous of me.'"

I could hear the lust in his voice as he continued, "You look so powerful when you use magic." My head was still spinning and I leaned against Dominic' shoulder. My magic seemed to be holding since no one was giving me funny looks anymore. If my spell worked as I hoped, then people who were jealous of me would simply not notice me.

By the time the teacher walked in, my head was settled. I still leaned against Dominic because the scent that seemed to radiate from him made me relax. I found myself ignoring the odd look I got from the teacher as he took his position behind his desk. I eventually sat up straight behind my desk but moved my hand onto Dominic' knee to maintain contact. His hand covered mine a few seconds later and he rubbed my hand gently as the class began. I told myself to remember to ask Dominic why the need for contact with him was so strong.

The biology itself was basic and I found that I kept up easily with the class. Today was more of a lesson reviewing the biology that they had learned previously this year and I had covered much of it before I moved here. I calmly listened and was bored with the class, wishing for it to be over. That was until I felt a pencil hit me on the back of my shoulder. I looked left to Dominic, who seemed distracted and I gently squeezed his leg as I felt something begin to grow inside me. He, once again, placed his hand over mine and rubbed it gently in a futile attempt to calm me. The ball of anger that was growing in my stomach did not lessen, no matter how hard I tried to concentrate on Dominic.

Once again, a pencil flew past my shoulder and my anger manifested itself as three words flew from my mouth, "Wiccecr^ft bordrand mec."

Dominic noticed my outburst and turned to look at me. I noticed the edges of his lips twitched with the beginning of a smile but disappeared as I rubbed my hand against his thigh, slowly creeping up his leg. He leaned forward and whispered into my ear as my hand edged closer towards his crotch, "You are insatiable, you know that?"

I muttered under my breath, knowing that his sensitive ears could pick it up, "And don't you love it. But, you're right, I'll save it for tonight." Another pencil flew towards my back before it stopped dead and rolled down it as my shield managed to absorb the force of it. I whispered to Dominic again, "If that person does it again, I am going to set him on fire and feed him to you. I am warning you!"

I felt his lips brush my cheek obviously trying to calm me down and no matter how hard I tried, I couldn't help the slight moan that escaped my mouth. The teacher was still facing the board, so I allowed myself a moment of indulgence before I pulled away from him and rested my head on my hands and my elbows on the desk. Soon the bell rang and I quickly escaped from the room, desperately trying not to cast magic again. I walked to my locker and dumped my biology books in it and grabbed my sports bag from it. I slammed my locker shut and rested my head on it.

A finger trailed along the back of my neck and I turned around and found Dominic looking down at me, "You need to relax because, if you get pissed off, you could hurt someone. And while I find it hot as hell when you are using your power, we must be careful that people don't start noticing 'strange' things happening around you. We should get to the gym now."

He leaned down and placed a kiss on my lips that was full of passion and pent-up lust. I could feel it in the way his body curved towards me, possessively, that he wanted me. I wanted him too, but now was not the time and we both knew that, so we headed to the gym. Gym passed by quickly, mainly because I didn't take my eyes off Dominic as we played basketball. I watched the way his arms moved, just a little too quick to be human as he blocked someone or shot the ball.

As soon as the gym was finished, we hit the showers and I had to use all of my concentration not to look at Dominic, because I knew the effect his naked body would have on me. I did notice how some of the other guys' eyes lingered on me as I walked away from the shower. I couldn't help it and spared one look back at Dominic, seeing his arse in all its glory.

Once I got dressed and walked outside, I headed to my next class without Dominic. I managed to find the classroom and survive the class. I distracted myself from missing him by thinking about the coming days.

Tomorrow was the last full day of the term before the summer holiday began for me. I pondered this as I dragged myself to my next class. A few people gave me looks as I walked towards my next class and a few made comments as I walked past them, but despite this, I stifled my anger and walked on.

CHAPTER 3

The day dragged on slowly and the comments from the others continued. The only thing that kept me from snapping was Dominic. Whenever I was about to snap, Dominic was somehow always there and he was like a ward against me losing it. However, he knew when to be there, I was grateful because I didn't want to snap and kill someone using my magic.

When lunch finally came, I walked towards the cafeteria and joined Dominic at a table close to the back wall. He had a tray of steaming hot food in front of him that was untouched. I had picked up a slice of pizza, some pasta, and some sort of yogurt. I sat down opposite him and grinned as I slowly began to eat. It was slightly disconcerting for me to eat while Dominic just sat there watching.

I decided that this was probably the best time to ask the questions that I had. Maybe then he wouldn't be as focused on me as I ate and I did have a lot of questions. I asked him, "How did Marcus know where you were? I thought you last saw him in 1940 or something?"He grinned, then said, "As my maker, his blood flows in my veins and that means that he can find me because I am his progeny. If you remember, I told you that if we mated, nothing could keep us apart. I said that no one could keep us apart and we would always be able to find each other because you would be my progeny."

I knew that my next question would touch a sore area, but I asked anyway, "If...if you made me, would he be able to find me?"

A shocked look crossed Dominic' face before he said slowly, "He would have a general idea as to your location, but not know exactly as I would."

All of my questions came to the surface in my mind at once. I continued, "If you made me, would it...would it hurt?"

I was surprised to see a look of anger on his face and it was reflected in his words also when he said, "It would and I will not put you through what I went through after I was turned."

I looked down scared by his reaction. His hand then moved to my chin and tugged it up so that my eyes met his. The anger was gone as he said, "Hey, I...I didn't mean to make you sad it's just that..." His voice trailed off then continued, "When you are first made there are very few things that hold your interest. You will feel wild and hyper all of the time. Blood will be your main desire but other needs will assert themselves as well. I was lucky. When Marcus made me, he was extremely strict and continually monitored me to make sure that I did not kill humans."

Thought immediately ran through my head.

"Would Dominic let me die so that I wouldn't have to face that?"

"Doesn't he want us to be together forever?"

"If I die and we are mates how would he live with himself, he said before it would destroy someone to lose their mate"

He smiled and I grinned weakly back, before changing I didn't want to express those questions yet. Maybe it was because I was afraid of the answers he may have given. Instead, I changed the topic, "How do you become your mate?"

He smiled and I grinned weakly back as he looked at me then said, "We would have to have sex and exchange blood soon after. It is the same way for two vampires as a vampire and a human."

I thought on that and then asked, "Has my taking your blood made some sort of link between us?"

He nodded, then said slowly, "I am able to sense your emotions and it strengthens our feelings for each other."

My mind moved quickly, thinking it explained why I trusted him already. But I didn't want to think that all the feelings were because of our link by blood.

"Was the love I felt for him because of the bond? Did he love Marcus?"

"What were you like when you were still human?" I asked hesitantly.

He smiled, but I could see the tension in his shoulders as he said, "It fades over time but I remember that I had private piano lessons and went to church in Dublin where I lived. I remember my sister and my mother and father. I loved running in the green fields near my aunt's house, but the individual details have faded."

I knew I had more questions but I wanted to digest all he had told me. Dominic took his turn to ask me questions. "What is your favorite Shakespeare play?"

I thought that an odd question out of all he could have asked, but quickly said, "Richard the Third, what's yours?"

He answered, "The Merry Wives of Windsor."

We continued to ask each other questions about likes and dislikes as we steadily learned more about one another.

I found out that his favorite piece of music was Allegri's Miserere. He described some of his travels around the world after 1948 when he thought Marcus had died. He visited Germany, Italy, Romania, Spain, France, China, and many other countries.

I listened intently to his stories. He had spent 64 years traveling after Marcus' supposed death.

I spoke as well and described some of my favorite pieces of music many of which were on the violin.

While Dominic was describing one of his many stories, I toed off my shoes and moved my leg under the table, and ran it up to his leg. He stuttered and whatever he was saying cut off. I moved my foot over his crotch, he leaned back in his chair and I slowly rubbed teasing circles with my foot.

He growled and I felt him go hard under his jeans.

I pulled away after a short minute because most people had left the cafeteria. I moved round to his side of the table and kissed him lightly on the lips. I smiled seeing how his eyes had grown slightly darker than their usual green.

Everybody seemed to know my name wherever I went in the school, the word seemed to have traveled fast, about how I had vanished with Dominic yesterday, and now seemed to give me a wide berth in class, that was apart from 1 boy who kept winking at me in class.

He was probably the one who kept throwing pencils at me, but my spell held out against it, but I did notice a slight drain in my strength each time a pencil collided with me, I considered spelling him but that seemed slightly drastic, I have no idea how to do any complex spells, and any of the powerful spells at my current skill level would probably kill me.

As I was walking towards my next class a boy walked into me and froze, I looked up to see a boy face to face with me, a buzz seemed to emanate from him when our skin touched, I looked up and his eyes locked with mine he exclaimed "you have magic, don't you".

I nodded then he smiled

"Hi I'm Niclaus a descendant of the Uthar coven, and might I ask from which coven you are descended?"

I thought for a second still trying to take in the information just presented to me

"I am a descendant of the Danaro coven and Hakara coven" his eyes widened in surprise when I said Danaro and even more so when I said Hakara, he whispered quickly

"I have never heard of someone descended from two powerful covens, the Danaro in itself is an extremely powerful coven but combined with their rival the Hakara, how long have you known you have had magic?"

"Less than a day"

"So new? But when I touched you I felt so much power, so powerful yet inexperienced, allow me to be the first from the Uthar coven to greet you, I have a warning for you, there is a blod drincere in the school he does not seem dangerous but I warn you that he would make a formidable enemy, judging by the amount of power you possess to him your blood would smell irresistible"

I laughed out loud

"I already know that there is a Vampire, I know him more intimately than you, in fact, it was his blood that awakened my magic"

I said, he looked as though I had just slapped him,

"I thought most people knew that I had been hanging around him but not everyone has."

I left him there with a look of shock on his face as I continued to my next lesson which was chemistry.

The class was half full when I arrived, and I took a seat towards the back of the classroom and waited for the class to begin, Dominic strolled in casually a god in flesh, he spotted me at the back of the classroom and strolled up to join me.

It hadn't been long since I had last seen him but It felt good to have him near me, his hand found mine and he rubbed soothing circles on the skin it, he leaned against my shoulder and moved towards my neck gliding his nose along the skin of it and inhaling.

He sighed in contentment before gently kissing my neck, he leaned back and caught my gaze, he whispered quietly "so hard to resist you have no idea, I just can't wait to bite into it again"

I laughed under my breath.

"Dominic if someone has magic does it change the taste of their blood?"

He nodded before saying, "some things change the taste of blood but magic has a more desirable taste than other causes. you are the sweetest that I have ever smelled, I am guessing that you have a lot of power at your disposal, you just need to learn how to channel it, but I will be with you to help you"

I thought about this for a second before continuing

"Are there any other witches at this school?"

A grimace crossed his face before he responded, "I have not been entirely honest, not only are there other witches but there Is a whole coven of them who migrated here from Russia 18 years ago. They are the Uthar coven, not the most powerful coven but not weak either, they are around 40 in number.

They tolerate me. but have made it clear to me that I should 'clean up my mess or face them.' What they do not know is that I am the governor of this area. I am in charge of keeping order among the younger vampires and to make sure that they clean up their mess."

"I met one of them, Niclaus he seemed nice, he said that he sensed my power when he touched me but

Dominic, why are you keeping such big things from me? You're the governor of the vampires in the area and didn't think I'd like to know that? I am surrounded by others who have magic, a whole coven full, and you didn't tell me. What else are you keeping from me? Do you have other progeny? I want to be your mate, but I want to make sure that I will be equal to you and that you will treat me like a mate and not a child."

Dominic lowered his head then his eyes flickered towards the door, Niclaus had just walked through the door, his eyes flickered around the room, they found me at the back of the classroom and I nodded at him, his eyes met Dominic and froze.

He began to move again a few seconds later and took a seat in the middle of the classroom, his shoulders remained tense until the teacher walked in and began our chemistry class.

The teacher was a middle-aged man beginning to go bald, short, and chubby. His voice seemed to match his appearance nasal in tone, "Right then, since this is our last full day I think we will have a more relaxed lesson. First, I believe we have a new student with us today." He looked down at his register to read my name, "Cayden Almer," he said raising his eyes to search the to the class for a new face.

I groaned as he looked around and I stood up and waited for the rest of the class to notice me. I wasn't surprised when the teacher called me to the front of the class. I spared one look back at Dominic before walking to the front of the classroom, where the teacher introduced himself as Mr. Hobbs and told me he was the head of the chemistry department. When I reached the front of the class, he asked me to introduce myself to the class.

"Hi, my name is Cayden I come from England as you can probably by my accent"

I answered a few more questions from Mr. Hobbs and then I returned to my seat at the back of the class. I was unsure why, but Dominic had a smug smile on his face when I sat down next to him, Mr. Hobbs had decided to watch a film for the lesson, he pulled the blinds and turned off the lights leaving the room in darkness.

In the darkness, I moved my hand towards Dominic, I knew he could see it, his eyes were better than any humans but it was the fact that the rest of the class could not see us was why I did it, my hand found his leg in the darkness.

I squeezed his leg affectionately feeling the cool skin beneath his jeans, he leaned back in his chair with his eyes closed, I ran my hand up to his leg slowly causing a low growl to emanate from his chest, my hand reached his upper thigh, each second coming closer to his crotch. When I reached it, he groaned a little too loudly and was rock hard beneath the fabric which was an achievement in his tight jeans, I leaned over and whispered in his ear, close enough that he felt my warm breath on the cold skin of his ear and neck "I just wanted to make sure you're ready for tonight I want tonight to be just between me and you".

I moved upwards to his jawbone while rubbing my hand over his cock.

I found his lips cold and soft, his hands moved to cup my face and pulled me closer towards him, his tongue pushed against my lips, I accepted him eagerly and sucked on his tongue coiling my own around it, his lips moved from mine and down to my neck.

I pushed him away a few minutes later and tried to slow down my heartbeat, his hand was over my chest a few moments later, feeling my heartbeat through my t-shirt, I sighed and leaned back in my chair as he rubbed my chest gently.

I leaned towards his face and then quickly moved and nibbled on his neck and then planted a kiss on top of it. We resumed our original positions as the film on the screen began to end and the lights came on. Dominic and I only remained in contact through our hands.

I pushed him away a few minutes later and tried to slow down my heartbeat, his hand was over my chest a few moments later, feeling my heartbeat through my t-shirt, I sighed and leaned back in my chair as he rubbed my chest gently.

I pulled his hand up to my face and pressed it against my cheek, he curved his hand around my face and his thumb stroked my cheekbone affectionately.

We resumed our original positions as the film on the screen began to end, the lights came on and I and Dominic only remained in contact through our hands.

We left the classroom and Dominic kissed me quickly on the cheek before he rushed off to his ethics class. I moved to my locker and dumped my books into it before I grabbed my geography books for my next lesson.

I was walking down the corridor toward my next class. I was running late and there was no one in the corridor except for three boys who were leaning against the lockers on the opposite side of the corridor from me.

Their eyes flickered to me as I walked past, the one in the middle was the leader of their group, his hair was greasy and off black, the other 2 looked like brothers with brown hair down to their collars, as I passed them the leader laughed and then said, "Fucking faggot, I see you found that gay prick, Dominic. If I had a chance I'd stick him in a hole and leave him to fucking rot"

I stopped dead, it was one thing to insult me, I was used to it but as soon as he insulted Dominic I immediately moved to the defensive and dropped my bag on the floor.

The walls on either side of me were lined with lockers, I felt confident that I could fight off 2 of them may be the third, I had spent the past four years slaving over my body in a gym, taking countless runs, and lifting weights. I was grateful for it because they had already begun to surround me. I knew I was in trouble because I still didn't know if my magic could help me. I wondered if Dominic could sense my concern. How would I get out of this?

I backed against the lockers and prepared to defend myself. I knew I couldn't fight them all.

One or two maybe but together I was easily outnumbered.

My conscious mind was chaotic. My subconscious however was planning. Words formed on my lips to protect me. His fist seemed to slow down and I wasn't sure whether it was the vampire blood in my system or my magic, but it helped, as his fist drew close to my face I muttered three words unconsciously:

'Waru fera mec"

His fist collided with my face, but I didn't feel it instead his fist seemed to stop dead.

He cried out in agony clutching his injured hand then said "What the hell! What the fuck are you?"

I know it may have sounded like a cliche but I could not help but respond by saying

"I am your worst nightmare" the 2 guys at the back, the two brothers, moved away.

Their eyes wide in shock and fear, they began to turn away, I extended my fingers into talons and extended one of my arms towards each of them and said.

"Alynian"

They froze on the spot their feet held to the floor.

One of them spat in my direction, I glared at him and called forth more magic, and said

"Ic creopere ^u"

Both of them fell to their knees,

The leader was trying to straighten himself up from his folded posture. He hand his fist clutched to his chest.

And he now tried to straighten himself to his full height.

A part of my brain seemed aware of the danger of someone seeing what was going on and I uttered under my breath:

"Ahydan us fram o^res "

That dealt with the possibility of others seeing us. I glared at the leader of their group and incanted;

"Ic bebindan   aet ^s flett"

He fell back onto the floor. I had used part of the same spell my mother had used on Dominic this morning but had instead bound this piece of human trash to the floor.

Human? I was not considering myself one of them.

"Now that you have seen what I can do you should know that I am capable of doing this any place, anywhere, so if I hear even one more snide comment about me or Dominic I will personally torture you in ways so horrible and painful they will push you to the precipice of insanity and hold you there, how about a slight demonstration hmm"

His words echoed back into my ears his threat against Dominic. Adrenaline and power were coursing through my veins. I felt so angry at them, they had insulted Dominic. He was mine and I would not allow anyone to comment on him. Inside my head, I accessed the darker part of my magic reserved for causing pain, the words flowed easily off my tongue

"Bryne eac adl"

They inhaled in shock and utter agony spread across their faces. They didn't cry out but the pain was evident on their faces and in the way their bodies writhed under my power.

"Ic tolysednes pu"

I muttered a few seconds later my compassion battling my anger. They gasped on the floor and I turned my back on them picked up my bag and walked off down the corridor and round a corner.

I walked into Dominic and he pulled me into his arms and kissed me gently on the lips. He pulled away earlier than I would have liked and said quickly "I tried to get here as fast as I could. I could feel your anger, it was coming off you in waves. What did they do to piss you off so much."

I looked down embarrassed, now that I thought back I had sort of overreacted but at the time I had felt so possessive and protective of Dominic. He put a hand under my chin and pulled my face upwards to catch his eyes, I spoke slowly embarrassed "They insulted you, and I..I.." he smiled then said "And what? Don't worry I won't get mad, I could never get angry at you."

"I protected myself from one of their punches and then I crippled the other 2 and forced them to their knees. bound them all to the floor and then I sort of...made them burn with pain..."

I trailed off expecting him to get mad at me even though he had promised not to.

He smiled then gave me a quick peck on the lips then said "This is slightly serious but nothing I can't handle. I will erase their memories later and plant a few false ones for them to find. But from the sounds of it, it seems that you don't need me to protect you all of the time."

I smiled at him and then said "I always need your protection, it feels good to have you so protective of me."

He laughed a quick chuckle and then said "Well after your last lesson meet me in my car and I will take you home and then. later I think we should go somewhere, a sort of date, then when we get back to my house..."

His hands moved to my arse and he pulled our groins into contact. I moaned at the intimate touch and then he continued.

"Well, we'll just see where we go from there. now I have to get back to class. so I shall see you later."

He kissed me quickly on the lips and then on my forehead before continuing past me and round the corner exclaiming as he did.

"You did do well with those guys, they're still on the floor".

I ran through the corridors to my next lesson which was geography, I was extremely late but luckily the teacher simply said before I could get a word out.

"I don't care, just sit down. listen and shut up"

I took a seat towards the front of the class next to a black girl and pulled my books out of my bag and looked up at the board.

The girl next to me began to speak.

"So you are Cayden right?"

I nodded half listening.

She continued speaking.

"So you are going out with Dominic right?"

I nodded again beginning to pay more attention to her and less to the work on the board which I noticed I had already studied.

She asked another question.

"Is he as hot topless as they all say?"

"Believe me I have seen him more than topless and I don't know what they all say but he is like a god on earth."

I blushed at my statement and looked down at my desk instead of at her, she began to say.

"Have you..." but was interrupted when the teacher said.

"Miss Thompson, do you have something to add to the class?"

"No Mr. Gilbertson, I'll pay attention from now on."

The lesson moved on to the geomorphology here in Virginia, I didn't know much about the city I now lived in. my mum had chosen Virginia because of the mild climate and had chosen the city of Hampton.

Phoebe kept her mouth shut for the rest of the lesson but I knew that she was bursting with questions.

I dodged that bullet however when at the end of the lesson everyone except me had homework to hand in, so I used that opportunity to slip away and dump my books in my locker. Most of the students had already left by the time I exited the building. I saw Dominic' car across the lot, I do not know much about cars. I had never really been interested In them, but the car that Dominic drove I had heard of, it was a black MR2. I faced it and rested on it while I waited for Dominic to arrive.

I was taken by surprise when a fist collided with the back of my head.

My face moved forward and hit the car. My temple collided with the side of the car and I went down a bright red light coloring the inside of my eyelids. I looked up to see the 3 people I had fought before, one of the 2 brothers placed a piece of duct tape over my mouth before kicking me in the stomach. I felt something give along with my ribs and I groaned into the tape.

The leader spoke down in my ear while the other kicked me in the stomach again.

"Try using that fucking shit again. I dare you. You haven't got Dominic to defend you either."

That was where he was wrong, I knew that Dominic could feel my fear and pain and I knew that he was coming for me. I curled into a ball as their onslaught continued to protect my face. I heard a growl in the distance, half-hidden in the darkness in my head.

I groaned under the tape as darkness consumed me.

Sometime later. I don't know how long someone pulled me up into a sitting position.

I exclaimed as I felt a searing pain spread through my arm and my ribs. I opened my eyes to meet Dominic'. The tape was gone from my mouth and I stared up at Dominic' green eyes.

He asked quickly obviously concerned.

"Cayden tell me where it hurts"

His fangs were descended but I ignored them as he moved his ear towards my mouth.

"My ribs and my arm" I managed to croak causing pain in my throat.

I felt his cool fingertips run up my arm and he gently squeezed assessing the damage. he reached my shoulder and I winced in pain. he muttered quietly.

'Dislocated shoulder"

He moved his hands to my ribs and gently pressed each one, he reached the bottom of the left half of my ribs and I cried out burning pain shooting through my chest.

"And 2 broken ribs" I heard him mutter.

Before he moved to my face, he gently rubbed my temple before pulling his wrist towards his face, his fangs dug into the flesh. His blood flowed sluggishly from the wound trickling down his wrist.

He moved it to my mouth, holding the back of my head supporting me against his body.

I sipped slowly knowing that it would remove the pain throughout my body. It went to work almost instantly beginning with the pain in my throat. I felt the blood begin to heal me by the tingling sensations that I felt around my body. My ribs seemed completely healed in a matter of seconds but the pain in my arm remained. Dominic whispered in my ear.

"I'm going to have to put your arm back into its socket. this is going to hurt. on 3. 1...2"

I felt a searing pain speed up my arm as Dominic put it back into its socket.

"3," he said once I had stopped wincing. pain painted all over his face.

He had removed his wrist from my mouth but I could not quite remember when. I had drunk quite a bit of the blood in his body. I guessed because his face seemed to have lost some of its colour, and his lips seemed a duller shade of red than before.

CHAPTER 4

His fangs remained descended as his eyes flicked towards the guy lying 10 feet away bleeding onto the pavement. My voice had returned and my pain had almost vanished. I grabbed Dominic's arm and pulled him towards me. he looked at me with hungry eyes. I spoke to him quickly.

"Dominic please just think, do you really want to drink that man's blood, after what he did to me."

This seemed to shock him out of his thirst-driven haze and his fangs slowly returned to their ascended state.

A look of extreme guilt crossed his face as he spoke.

"If I had erased their minds of you earlier, this would not have happened. If only I had been thinking logically, this..."

'Sshh" I said and leaned forward weakly and pecked him lightly on the lips. Noticing the lightening of his eyes as I did so.

"I'm going to be fine."

A single blood tear rolled down his which I brushed away, hesitating to stroke his cheek briefly.

He grinned down at me and pulled me up onto my feet and opened the car door for me and helped me get in.

My legs felt weak but I was sure that soon his blood would have me back to normal. In a second he was in the driver's seat, he reached over to the glove compartment, opened it, and pulled out a blood bag. He stared at it in his hands with a look akin to shame. I saw his fangs descend and he bit into the bag and quickly drained the contents. after he had he looked at me looking slightly embarrassed.

I smiled at him and then said.

"It must have been hard not drinking that humans' blood when It was spilling over the pavement. I think I have been taking too much out of you, when you get home you should feed."

He nodded curtly then responded saying.

"I'm sorry you had to see me like that. My anger coupled with my hunger threw me off guard.

With you feeding off me. my hunger... almost drove me over the edge. I will fill myself up on blood bags before I take you out tonight. at least that way you could drink from me if you want and I would be in full control of my urges."

I ran my hand up to his leg and then said already feeling better.

"I hope you still have those urges though, they may come in handy later."

His eyes turned to me full of warmth as he leaned forward and kissed me. My hands made their way to his neck pulling him closer. He broke away for a few seconds and then moved his seat back as far as it would go then moving at blinding speed pulled him onto him.

My legs were on either side of his and I leaned down and kissed him quickly on the lips then moved down his face to his neck. he kissed up my neck and then his right hand pulled my face up to his and he kissed me with passion, his tongue tapped my lips seeking entrance.

I opened my mouth and accepted him trying not to notice the taste of metal in his mouth from the blood bag.

While I was distracted by his mouth his left hand found my hard cock in my trousers and squeezed me. I broke away from his lips moaning as he rubbed me through my trousers. he had moved up to my arms met by his right and he moved so fast that I did not see it.

We ended up on the back seat with his lying on top of me.

"You have no idea how much I have wanted this all day, your hands my leg have made me want you moaning in pleasure, now I have my chance."

His hands ran down my t-shirt towards my trousers, his hands found my dick beneath the fabric, he rubbed me before quickly undoing the button and the zip and pulling them down to my ankles. He pulled out his car keys and pushed a button on them and the front windscreen turned dark along with the side and rear windows cutting us off from the rest of the world.

He ran his hands over my cock and I moaned, his hands were making wonderful friction between my cock and the fabric of my boxers. His hands moved to the waistband of my boxers and his thumb traced the waistband. I locked my legs around his hips as he began to rub my cock, he tugged at the waistband of my briefs releasing my cock from its prison.

He asked me quickly

"Could I...feed, I won't take much" I hesitated and then said after I had assessed my strength.

Sure.'

He kissed my inner thigh and then said.

"I don't usually feed on the groin but from my experience, it is quite exhilarating."

His fangs descended and I tensed up as he leaned forward towards my left thigh. He moved his hands to my hips and gently massaged the flesh. I relaxed immediately, whatever he was massaging at my hips was sending waves of relaxation up my body. He kissed the flesh of my inner thigh inhaling deeply against my skin.

He ran his fangs lightly across the skin, kissed it then gently bit into my thigh. I gasped. this was far more pleasurable than when he fed on my neck. the pleasure seemed to move upwards and I soon found myself moaning as he fed on me.

His right hand secure my thigh while his left moved up towards my cock, I moved my hand into his hair and tugged gently on it. his hand reached my cock and he slowly held me and wanked my cock while he fed, the pleasure was indescribable both his feeding and his hand on my cock were driving me over the edge, I was on the verge of cumming and he knew it he pulled away from my thigh and moved upwards towards my face his teeth still stained with my blood.

He kissed me on my tired lips, I lowered my head back to the seat as he sped up his left hand on my cock. My hips began to thrust into his hand, a few seconds later I felt his mouth lock over the tip of my cock. My vision colored with white streaks as I came into his mouth.

I breathed heavily as he leaned back onto the floor, his lips gently moved to my thigh again.

He licked the wound and then I saw him pull one of his fingers up to his fangs. He pierced the flesh and a small droplet of blood oozed from the flesh, he rubbed it over the bite wounds and I watched the flesh heal in seconds.

I reached down and pulled up my boxers and then my trousers, I moved back to the passenger seats and then Dominic returned to the driver seat and pulled his seat forward again.

He turned to me a look of satisfaction on his face, I turned in my seat and leaned in forward, and kissed him gently on the lips, he smiled as I pulled away.

"I'm sorry I forgot about your needs it was just so..."

His smile grew wider and he cut me off.

"Don't worry it was satisfying you, but don't worry we still have all night."

One of his hands moved to my face and he stroked my cheek before I asked him.

"So where are we going tonight?"

"Most of my kind are quite old and have instituted themselves into society, they mainly choose to own bars, one such bar is reserved for specific clients. If I took you there it would show to the others that I dare to openly love a human.

Do you remember when I told you about the Uthar coven?"

I thought back and remembered him saying something about being a governor for this area.

"Yeah you said something about governing the area"

He nodded and then said.

"Yes, well most of my subjects as it saw humans only as food, if I showed them that I had taken a human as my mate, it might change some of their views. Most of the Vampires under my rule are around a century old or younger, they respect me because I am their elder but also because I am their governor".

I tried to envision Dominic as a governor but found it too funny to contemplate. I started laughing and watched the expression on Dominic' face turned quizzical.

'Why are you laughing?" He asked me.

I managed to stop myself after a few more seconds of laughter then responded.

"I'm just trying to envision you as a governor"

He smiled and then said.

"I was made a governor in 1923 when I was 139, all that it means is that in any area that I choose to live I have the ability to enact judgment on any vampire or other supe who threatens to expose us to humans...or any humans who threaten to find out about us. I am also responsible for keeping track of all vampires and finding them if they go missing."

He had started the car and then began to drive out of the parking lot, "Do you have some sort of government or hierarchy? Who is the leader of your kind?"

He hesitated for a second and I quickly said "I'm sorry if you can't tell me I understand"

He shook his head.

"I'm allowed to tell you anything and everything as a supe yourself, but if you tell a human, I would have to kill them or me" He trailed off.

"Does this break one of your laws, what we have?" I asked

He shook his head and then said.

"No, it could, if I thought you would tell anyone about my kind. But as a supernatural yourself I don't think you would risk telling anyone. Some of my kind however disagree with vampires dating humans, most simply see you as food.

Some fall in love with humans but are afraid that they could kill them, some of the older vampires however are capable of controlling their urges, and are capable of feeding without harming the human.

Take you, for example, if a younger vampire were to feed off you, they would find it more difficult to stop themselves with you than with another human without magic. You are in danger more from a younger vampire than from an older one." he broke off a small smile present on his lips.

"Your blood provides us with greater sustenance than a normal human. I am surprised that you have not already fallen prey to a vampire, even before you unlocked your magic you still smelled irresistible."

He paused judging my reaction to it then continued.

"And as for our leader and government, it is slightly complicated, each continent has a monarch, usually an old vampire older than 900 years."

"So who is the monarch of North America?"

A grimace crossed his face before he responded.

"His name is Ioannes, he was turned around 500bc in Greece. He is the 2nd oldest vampire known to exist, he is over 2500 years old and lives in Norfolk.

It was one of the reasons why I chose to live here, with a monarch so close it is one of the most carefully monitored areas in America, he personally requested that I take charge of this area as soon as I moved here." 1 thought back to the look on his face when I mentioned the monarch.

"Do you have a problem with him?" he turned his head then said.

"When I was made a governor it meant that any monarch could call me into their service. I have been around for 228 years and have met 4 of the monarchs 2 women and 2 men, women were the queens of South America and North Africa and the King of Europe.

Ioannes the King of North America likes to keep an eye on me".

"Why does he want to keep an eye on you?" I asked, he looked down and sighed before meeting my gaze and saying hesitantly.

"He tried to...he asked me if...." he stopped and I asked him.

"He asked you to what?" he locked eyes with mine and then it hit me.

"He asked you to be his mate!" I shouted at him.

"Yes, but I turned him down. Unfortunately, his interest in me has not faded over the past 30 or so years. But once the word gets around that I am with you, he will probably summon us. I think he will be quite interested to know that my mate is a human" he answered pleadingly.

I fell onto the defensive and said to him.

He can summon us?

Dominic nodded and slowly responded.

"Whilst I reside in his territory I am technically his subject. Whilst I was in England before I started traveling in 1946, King Zachariah of Europe summoned the governors to help combat a threat to our kind. A group of half-crazed Fae."

I cocked an eyebrow to this but could tell from the setting of his jaw that it was a closed subject.

"Does Ioannes have the power to force you to leave me" I half-whispered the words afraid of his answer.

"No, he cannot, that is one of our most sacred of laws, a monarch cannot force a vampire to give up his mate" he pulled my face up and smiled at me.

I leaned forward and kissed him on the lips. The thought of whoever this Ioannes guy was, taking

Dominic away from me filled me with anger. Dominic was mine and I was his.

Dominic put his hand on my neck and said

"Cayden, you are mine and I am yours. that is not going to change. just calm down I won't leave you. now I will meet you in an hour, I'd leave a note for your mum, she is protective of you,.most of the humans, I know who date vampires have been kicked out by their parents. don't worry she will get used to me. I hope".

I gave him a quick kiss on the lips, opened the car door, and walked towards my house, I looked back to see him waving before revving his engine and driving off down the street.

I pulled out my front door keys and opened the door. I walked upstairs and stepped into the bathroom. I kicked off my shoes and socks and turned started to run myself a bath.

While my bath was running I moved into my room and tried to figure out what I should wear. If I was going out with Dominic. I decided on a v-neck white t-shirt that would expose my neck (I knew that that would attract a lot of attention) and a pair of blue Levi jeans.

I grabbed my clothes and walked back to the bathroom. I tested the water before I stripped and stepped in. I laid back in the water and felt my muscles relax completely. The warm water seemed to be drawing out all of my anxiety and tension and leaving me in a completely relaxed state.

I leaned back and closed my eyes enjoying the feeling of the warm water against my skin.

I trailed my hand down my body gently pinching my nipples before continuing down.

My cock began to harden still under the influence of Dominic' blood. The sensations shot up my body and I slowly began to rub. By this point my cock was hard and I started to wank my cock with quick forceful movements.

A few minutes later just as I was on the verge of cumming I heard a voice say.

Mmm, delicious I find myself hard just watching you.

My eyes shot open at the first syllable and I sat up quickly in the bath to find Marcus standing there. He was staring down at me with a glint in his eyes. His black hair shook as he laughed at my response.

I tried to cover myself from his gaze and stepped out of the bath which let me tell you isn't easy sporting a hard-on. I looked at the hook on the wall and felt terror shoot through me as I saw I had forgotten to get a tcwel. I vainly tried to cover my hard cock as I racked my brain for a spell to hide my naked body from his eyes. I looked up at him quickly and saw his eyes trail down my body.

I quickly said.

"Ahydan min pintel fram Marcus"

I felt a tingling sensation on my cock and hoped I had just hidden it from Marcus' eyes.

I looked up at him and demanded.

"Why the fuck are you here?"

He smiled and then said.

"I may not be gay but Dominic does have taste, and as to the reason for my visit I require yours and Dominic' assistance."

I was still pissed at him and glared daggers in his direction while I said.

"Well then why didn't you just go to his house and ask him?"

He laughed again then said.

"Because Dominic tried to help me last night but was unable to assist me further than I already achieved. We are both governors of the vampire world and an important vampire has gone missing.

I pulled an image from the mind of a human that he and some scientist trapped this vampire.

They are currently experimenting on him to discover what he is and how he works.

I have recently learned that you are a quite powerful witch, and your skills would be greatly appreciated in this matter"

Focusing on keeping my power flowing to the spell I said.

"Why is this vampire so important? This is personal to you isn't it?"

He stiffened then said quietly.

"Clever. You would be correct he is. The reason being is that he is my maker. I would die to protect him."

"Alright I will try to help you, but could we do it tomorrow afternoon. Dominic and I have already made plans for tonight but I will do what I can to help you tomorrow. Now could you go away, it is slightly disturbing that you walk in on me while I am naked in the bath. I thought you had a mate"

He smiled and then said.

"Yes I have my own mate, but as one of my friends a few centuries ago said 'there is nothing wrong with window shopping, though I prefer women I have had my share of men and none have been quite as...desirable as you though.

If I had found you before Dominic I may not have been restrained as he was and now I will bid you farewell."

He moved away with incredible speed and I relaxed as soon as I heard my front door open and close.

I released the spell and returned to my bath, I washed my hair and after a few more minutes of attempted relaxation, I gave up and got out of the bath. Marcus had given me something to worry about, what if another vampire had found me before Dominic, I would probably be dead in a dumpster somewhere drained of every last drop of blood.

About 20 minutes had passed from the time I walked through the door and got into my outfit for the night. I felt full of energy after the large amount of blood that I had drunk from Dominic, it also had the side effect of making me horny as hell. And let me tell you me hyper is bad enough. Hyper AND horny never a good combination.

I walked into the kitchen and ruffled through the drawers looking for a pad and pen.

I quickly scribbled a note.

"Mum I'm going out for the night and yes it is with Dominic.

I'll probably be back late or not at all so don't wait up for me."

At the bottom, I added.

"And don't worry he may not be your ideal type of person for me but I really like him."

I was careful in case someone read the note, and deliberately avoided anything supernatural.

By the time Dominic knocked on my door I was beginning to go stir crazy, he strolled in through the front door. He was wearing a tight pair of jeans and a black shirt with a leather jacket on top. All in all his clothing emphasized his best features. His defined thighs are the bulge of his pecs leading up to his broad shoulders.

He was humming a lively tune and I asked.

"What are you humming it sounds nice"

"A little song that was written around 80 years after I became a vampire in Ireland" He replied a brief second later.

"What's it called?" I asked.

He replied alluringly a small smile present on his lips "I'll tell me ma, now enough of that come here"

He pulled me into his arms, smiled widely then said "I missed you"

He leaned forward and kissed my forehead. I looked up at his face and noticed how he looked more radiant than an hour ago and his lips were more red than before.

"You fed" I commented He nodded then smiling said.

"I wanted to make sure I won't lose control, and now I have more than enough blood in me for you in case you get injured or.."

He trailed off and his hands ran down my back to my arse which he squeezed affectionately.

"For other activities".

I beamed up at him and leaned forward to kiss him on the lips. His hands-on my arse tugged me closer into his body bringing our cocks into contact. I ran my hands up his chest to the lapels of his leather jacket and tugged him against me.

He pulled away and said as and took one of my hands.

"Don't worry. They'll be time for that later."

I sighed annoyed but thought forward envisioning the night ahead. He led me through the front door. We walked down the short path to the road I looked for his MR2 but could not see it anywhere. I turned to him when we reached the road and asked.

"Where's your car?"

He shook his head then said.

"We're not driving" he pointed into the distance and said "The sun has almost set and my speed and strength are already much stronger, I'm going to carry you'

I looked at him in disbelief then asked "So where are we going, where is this bar?"

He responded almost immediately.

"In Norfolk, around 16 miles away give or take"

I had seen his strength and speed so I doubted it would take us long to get there but I asked anyway.

"How long will it take us to get there?"

He looked up in thought for a second and then said "3 minutes probably less".

I grinned at him and he grinned back, he let go of my hand and in the space of time it took me to blink I was in his arms, he smiled at me and then said "You are so warm, it must be off-putting to be near something so cold?"

I shook my head then to show my point I leaned In close and wrapped my arms around his neck.

I kissed my way up his face then caught his gaze and then said.

"To me, I don't mind that you're skin is cold because I know that in here"

I moved my right hand over his heart.

"Is so much love and warmth and I have always preferred being cold to being hot".

He grinned cheekily then said "Well for someone who hates being hot you sure are doing a good job of it."

He smiled lovingly at me and then he was running. Up until that point I had not truly gauged his speed. He was a ghostly bullet whizzing through the city and within a minute we were in the country.

I leaned my head against his shoulder and just enjoyed the feel of the breeze against my skin. All too soon he stopped. I opened my eyes and found myself in an alleyway, Dominic lowered me to the floor commenting on my choice of clothes.

"It's going to be hard to keep you to myself what with you smelling so good and looking even better, especially when you're displaying the veins on your neck so prominently."

He grinned at me before offering me his hand, I took it and he led me out of the alley way and into the streets of Norfolk.

It was beginning to drizzle as we walked through the streets, skyscrapers were on either side of us and I was beginning to wonder where exactly this bar was, he continued to pull me through the streets a smile fixed on his face, we reached an alley way on our left and he tugged me down it towards a door at the end.

A woman was leaning against the door examining her nails. She looked up as we approached and stared at Dominic, She smiled at him, and then her eyes turned to me and she cocked her head before turning to Dominic and saying "Dominic it has been a while since you were last here, it's good to see you though, your presence should keep the order, so who is your date?"

Dominic tugged me forward, I had been half-hidden behind him apprehensive of speaking to the vampire, he said to her while her eyes roamed over me.

"This is Cayden, he is my mate"

A look of shock crossed the woman's face before it was replaced with curiosity.

"A human, strange, he smells..." she inhaled deeply to accentuate her point.

"Sweet" she finished.

Dominic smiled and then said "He is a witch, that was what drew me to him at first, even before his magic awakened, he still smelled incredible."

She smiled at Dominic then at me before asking me "Could you do me a favor and stop this rain, it's starting to mess with my hair"

I looked at Dominic and he nodded.

I closed my eyes and tried to think of words to stop the rain. I cobbled together something I thought would stop it. I hesitated then continued.

"Ic beclyse ^m heofon ond alynian ^m ren" I said quietly.

The rain slowed till it was only spitting and then ceased altogether.

I opened my eyes and smiled at the woman before she said "Thank you."

She pulled a key out of her pocket and opened the door behind her, she motioned for us to go through and Dominic pulled me through and into the corridor.

After the door behind us had closed he turned to me and said "She didn't really want you to stop the rain she just wanted to see if you were a witch."

I looked at him and asked as we continued to walk down the corridor.

"Why did she want to know?"

He shrugged and then said "She will probably tell Ioannes about you. He is her maker. He will probably come running if I know him as well as I think I do. He will come to find out what his competition is."

That made me angry. I said in a bubble of fury "Why the fuck does he want to find out about me, and why is he still interested in you after you've turned him down, does he need to have it spelled out for him, you are not interested in him, and secondly you are mine, you chose me."

I had no idea why I was getting so angry but the thought of someone trying to take Dominic away from me was a tender area.

He stopped and grabbed me around the waist and shoved me against the corridor wall, his lips pressed against mine and his tongue pushed past my lips and assaulted my mouth, his hands ran up my chest. My anger evaporated replaced by lust. As his arm pulled our groins into contact.

I was about to put my hands on his neck when he pulled away and looked into my eyes.

"Cayden relax, I am not going to leave you and I hope I just proved that I chose you."

He kissed me again and I grabbed his jacket and pulled him closer. I heard the door we had walked through at the end of the corridor open and footsteps echoed through the hall.

Dominic pulled away and led me along the corridor. I glanced back at the person behind us. It was a woman but I could not see her face clearly, I moved closer to Dominic and he put his arm around my shoulders.

We reached the end of the corridor and he pulled open the door at the end and revealed the club inside. The walls were black and red and there seemed to be quite a lot of people inside. A breeze blew from behind me, I saw half a dozen people directly in front of me inhale deeply. Their eyes collectively grew darker as I watched. I clutched Dominic' hand and he led me into the club. His eyes roamed over the people in the bar visibly warning them that I was his.

94

THE END

Other Books by Sir Patrick Bijou

- CRYPTOCURRENCY: THE NEXT LEVEL FOR BANKING REFORM
- SPECIAL DRAWING RIGHTS (SDR) VOLUME 2
- SPECIAL DRAWING RIGHTS (SDR) AND THE FEDERAL RESERVE
- MYSTIC AGENT
- PRIVATE PLACEMENT PROGRAMS: THE HOLY GRAIL
- WILDFLOWER
- WILDFLOWER: SECOND EDITION
- PARANORMAL CLUB
- FINANCIAL INTELLIGENCE: FUNDAMENTALS OF PRIVATE PLACEMENT PROGRAMS (PPP)
- OFFENCE AND JUSTICE
- ENCHANTED SOUL
- LETHAL LEGACY: THRILL OF THE HUNT
- LETHAL LEGACY: THRILL OF THE HUNT 2
- THE BLUEPRINT TO INTELLIGENT INVESTORS
- A MODEL FOR MURDER
- MAKE MONEY DOING NOTHING
- THE GOOD TASTE
- UNDYING LUST
- ETERNAL LOVE
- GUIDE TO PRIVATE PLACEMENT PROJECT FUNDINGTRADE PROGRAMS: UNDERSTANDING HIGH-LEVEL PROJECT FUNDING TRADE PROGRAMS
- KARMIC LOVE
- BEGINNERS OF NOWHERE
- UNDERCOVER

- UNLOCKING THE SECRETS OF BITCOIN AND CRYPTOCURRENCY: CRYPTO CURRENCY MADE EASY
- HOW TO TRADE DERIVATIVES AND CFDS TO MAKE MILLIONS PAPERBACK
- KARMIC LOVE
- SECRET OF WEALTH CREATION: PRINCIPLE LESSONS ON THE SECRETS OF BUILDING A LONG LASTING WEALTH
- CRYPTOCURRENCY MILLIONAIRE: MAKE MONEY WITH CRYPTOCURRENCY AND EAU-COIN
- HOW TO TRADE DERIVATIVES AND CFDS TO MAKE MILLIONS
- UNLOCKING THE SECRETS OF BITCOIN AND CRYPTOCURRENCY: CRYPTO CURRENCY MADE EASY
- GUIDE TO PRIVATE PLACEMENT PROJECT FUNDING TRADE PROGRAMS: UNDERSTANDING HIGH-LEVEL PROJECT FUNDING TRADE PROGRAMS
- SECRET OF WEALTH CREATION: PRINCIPLE LESSONS ON THE SECRETS OF BUILDING A LONG LASTING WEALTH